The author of the Flipping Numbers series

PRESENTS

Naughty Housewives 2

Ernest Morris

Good 2 Go Publishing

Naughty Housewives 2

Written by Ernest Morris
Cover Design: Davida Baldwin
Typesetter: Mychea
ISBN: 9781943686544

Copyright ©2016 Good2Go Publishing
Published 2016 by Good2Go Publishing
7311 W. Glass Lane • Laveen, AZ 85339
www.good2gopublishing.com
https://twitter.com/good2gobooks
G2G@good2gopublishing.com
www.facebook.com/good2gopublishing
www.instagram.com/good2gopublishing

Acknowledgments

FIRST AND FOREMOST, GOD (Allah) please continue to direct me on the right path so that I can not only become a vessel that you work through, but also someone that others can become inspired by. Amen!!

Life's journey has taken me to places that made me sit back and question what I am really here for and why this is happening to me. I had to really evaluate myself and realize that all the negative things that have happened to me had a sole purpose. It was to change me from a lil boy to a man. Just 'cause I'm an adult doesn't mean I was living like one.

Here's something people never knew about me: When I lost my mother (Jacqueline Morris) when I was fourteen, and then my sister (Conyia Morris) a year later, I went into a state of depression. I even contemplated suicide. People always saw E.J. smiling on the outside, but inside, I was a complete wreck emotionally, as well as spiritually. I thought how could there be a God if he took two of the most important people in my life away from me. There are times when I am alone and I think about my mom and sister, and I tear up because I miss them so much. Even till this day I still do. I now realize, though, everyone is born with an expiration date. God (Allah) has a bigger plan for every one of us. I love you Mommy and Connie; REST IN PEACE!

Anyway, what I'm trying to say is, it took me all these years to see and reach my full potential in life. A man without a vision for his future will always return to his past. I'm not going backward, I'm moving forward. I can't no longer be that person I used to be. You will get to know the real me in my autobiography, *One Man's Triumph*, coming soon.

I was blessed with four beautiful children: Le'Shea Burrell, Sahmeer Morris, Demina Johnson, and Shayana Morris, and I never really had the chance to be in their lives because of my actions in the past. Any man can make a baby, but it takes a real man to step up and be a father. I wasn't that man. I want them to know that I'm gonna spend the rest of my time left on this earth, with some help from them, to be a good, if not great, father. There is a light at the end of the tunnel, and I'm heading toward it.

I dedicate this book to not only my children, but also their mothers: Brandi Burrell, Kendra Funchez, Meena Johnson, and Nakisha Cousin, for being the strongest women I ever have known, and for their unconditional motherly love. Y'all sacrificed every-thing to raise the best children in the world. If it was up to me, every day would be Mother's Day.

I also dedicate this book to my brothers: Kevin (Chubb) Morris and Sedric (Walid) Morris. We never had the brotherly bond we were supposed to have, because we were always apart, but time heals all wounds.

To all my extended family: Loveana, Cynthia, Theresa, Kita, Trina, Gianni, Dwunna, Leneek, Kimmy, Alona, Lyric, Jamie, Zyrinah, Dom, Pam, Nyia, Myra, Symira, Jigga, Neatra, Dee Dee, Sharon, Aleesha, Damein, Nafeese, Shy, Phylis, Shot Gun, Eric, Sherman, Eddie, Maurice, Rasheed, Frank, Ty, Donte, Chris, Ed, Vettie, Torey, Zy, Arnold, Christian, Baheem, Gavin, Nay Nay, Renea, Tia, Sherry, Shawn, Seiara, Layah, Ci Ci, etc. Thank you for your support in making me a better man.

To all my aunts and cousins: Peggy, Katherine, Cathy, Mildred, Sister, Tee, Cindy, Bobby, Steve, June, Gilbert, Wade, Ottis, Lil Man, Fat Man, Meka, Antoinette, Sinky, Vanessa, Glenda, Sareeta, Mike Mike, Stephenie, Brandy, Pooh, Link, Cinquetta, The Twins, Jacon, Tasha, Bo, Dee,

Tysheka, Barry, Pooch, Angie, Meek, Eric, James, Ronald, Keith, Tony, Michael, Darnell, Toga, Chrissy, Brenda, Tranea, Felicia, Nygel, Auntie, Peanut, Janell, Loretta, Ray, Etta, Nikki, Mike, Danielle, Kenyetta, Stanetta, Rasheeda, G.I., Margaret, Rubar, etc. There are so many of you that I know I am forgetting, and I apologize for it. I really want to thank all of you for just being the people you are. My eyes are open, and now I truly see what everyone means to me.

To my best friends: Yahnise, Harmon, you already know that words cannot explain your loyalty to me, and mine to you. Keep doing your thing, ma, and let the haters keep hating.

To everyone at the Cheesecake Factory: A.J. Katz, John, Shelly, Arnold, Kayla, Marcus, Jade, Will, Evani, Lope, Dom, Rhonda, Christina, Pamela, Janette, Morgan, Tia, Jalisa, Ty, Bill, London, Melissa, Toya, Stacks, Dawn, Sarah, Torey Jackie, Stacy, Ryan, Leanne, Edward, Nestor Nancy (both), Mia, and everyone else that I missed—you know who you are—thanks for letting me be a part of the winning team.

I want to give a shout out to all my Passyunk family. They took the buildings but left the name, memories, and love.

To Omar, Piper (Pike), and Knowledge (South Philly), that door is about to open up to those prison walls. It just takes patience and hope. Each one of you inspired me in different ways. I want you to know that I will never forget you. Stay strong in there, and I will see you on the other side when we hit those Passyunk reunions up.

Special thanks to Worlds and Josh for staying on me to complete this. I hope that this will be another great one.

ON PAPER, ONCE AGAIN I have turned a vision in my head into a reality on paper. It started with Flipping Numbers, and it won't stop until I have reached out to the minds and hearts of everyone across the world. Naughty Housewives is one of my toughest challenges because it made me have to think outside the box and create characters that would make you visualize yourself as being.

I thank God first and foremost, for blessing me with this gift of being able to write novel after novel and continuing to do it successfully. No one knows the struggle that writers go through to constantly put out storylines that will keep readers intrigued and wanting more. It truly takes time and dedication, and I, along with the other authors, appreciate your support.

Thank you so much!!

Naughty Housewives 2

Ernest Morris

One

HE FELT HER STARTING to become attached, and that's something he couldn't have. They were cooped up in the Hilton Hotel after a long night of steamy sex, watching a rerun of *The Big Bang Theory.*

"I'm about to take a shower. Would you like to join me?" she asked, grabbing his penis, trying to stroke it back to life.

"Keep doing that, and we may not even make it that far," he joked, squeezing her breasts together.

Katie let out a soft moan as her pussy began to moisten from his firm grasp. Just as she thought things were about to heat up, Kevin released his grip. He hopped out of bed and started putting his clothes back on. Katie tried to grab his arm but missed.

"Where are you going? I thought we were going to chill here for the night. You're not going to leave me here with a wet pussy are you?" she asked.

"I can't stay tonight because my wife will be waiting up for me at home. We can get together this weekend when I go out of town. It will just be you and me. Does that sound good to you?" he said, leaning over and biting her nipple.

"Ouch, don't do that. You can't be putting any marks on me. Anyway, I guess that would be cool. Don't stand me up again like you have been doing lately. I might have to give the misses a call and tell her what's going on." She smirked.

"You better not do nothing stupid like that," he replied, watching her sprawled out over the bed. She was looking sexy as hell in her birthday suit. The smell of sex still lingered in the air.

"Shut up, you know I was just playing. I know how to play my position. I hope you do."

Kevin smiled at her as he grabbed his car keys off the nightstand and headed toward the door. Although she was smiling, he had a feeling that she was serious. Even if she wasn't, he knew he had to stop seeing her before it got too serious.

When he reached his car, he tried calling Marcus a couple of times to let him know he was heading home. When he kept getting his voicemail, he decided to leave a message. He figured that they had probably fallen asleep after their long night. He headed home, hoping that Michelle was asleep so he could hop right in the shower. He didn't take one look back at the hotel because he knew what would happen if he did.

It was precisely 3:00 a.m. when Kevin turned onto his block and found a bunch of police cars and an ambulance in front of his house. He came to a quick stop and jumped out of the car. As he was heading toward the front door, two officers stopped him.

"I'm sorry, sir, but you can't go in there right now. This is a crime scene," one of the officers said.

"This is my house. My wife and son are in there. What's going on?"

A detective at the scene heard the commotion and walked over to where they were standing. He pulled out his wallet, displaying his credentials, and flashed it at Kevin.

"I'm Detective Davis, and your name is?" he asked, tucking his wallet back into his pocket.

"My name is Kevin Wright. Now are you going to tell me what the hell is going on and why they won't let me go inside?"

"There has been a murder, Mr. Wright. I'm sorry, but your wife was shot twice in the chest at close range. She died instantly. You will not be able to go in there until CSI finishes conducting their preliminary investigation and clears the scene."

Kevin didn't hear anything after "murder." He felt his whole world come crashing down in an instant. His knees got weak, and he fell to the ground as tears released from his eyes.

"Who, what, when?" was all he could say.

The detective kneeled down beside him trying to comfort him, but it was no use. Kevin jumped up and tried to force his way through the officers to get to his wife.

"Get off of me. I want to see her. Let me go," he yelled out, to no avail. The officers were too strong for him. He sat back down on the ground.

"Someone broke into your house trying to rob it, but was surprised to see your wife still up. When she came down the steps, the burglar must have panicked and shot her twice in the chest. Your son heard the shots and ran to his mother's aid but was also struck in his arm before the burglar ran from the house empty-handed. Your wife was pronounced dead at the scene, and your son was rushed to the hospital. While they're processing the scene, I can take you over to see your son," the detective said, helping Kevin up and over to his car.

Detective Davis couldn't sense any signs of guilt on Kevin's face during the ride to the hospital. All he saw was a grieving man, taking the death of his wife very hard. On the way there, Detective Davis asked him a few questions like his whereabouts, what time he left, and when the last time he talked to her was. Even though they were routine questions that had to be asked, Kevin felt offended. When they arrived at the emergency entrance, Kevin ran through the doors to find his son.

"I'll be out here if you need me, Mr. Wright," the detective yelled out to him as the doors shut behind him.

When Kevin walked into the room and saw that his son was okay, it felt like a big burden had been lifted off his shoulders. The bullet had gone straight through, just missing an artery. After comforting his son for the next three hours, Kevin decided to return home and try to figure out what had happened.

~ ~ ~ ~

When he finally made it home, there was still some police activity, but not as much as when he first arrived earlier. He walked in, looking around to make sure nothing was missing. After observing that everything was in its rightful place, he walked over toward the staircase. He looked down at the bloodstain still embedded in the carpet, and reality kicked in. He kneeled down and started crying. The pain he was feeling at that time was unbearable.

"Bang, bang, bang! Kevin open the door. We know you're in there," Marcus said, continuing to knock on the door.

Kevin wiped his face and then went to answer the door. He let Marcus and Sasha in. Sasha looked like she had been crying for hours, the way her mascara was running off her face. Marcus looked

7

like he was ready to go to war. His eyes were bloodshot red. They walked in, gave Kevin a hug, and then sat down on the couch.

"I'm so sorry for your loss. If you need me to do anything, just say it, and it's done," Marcus whispered in his ear.

From the look on Marcus's face, no words needed to be spoken to know exactly what he was insinuating. All Kevin did was nod his head, then walk over to the bar.

"I appreciate that, and trust me, you'll be the first one I call when the time is right. Would y'all like something to drink?" he asked, pouring himself some Scotch.

"Let me get a shot of henney," Marcus replied.

"I'll take a glass of Moet, please," Sasha stated.

"Okay."

He made their drinks; then they sat and talked for a while, trying to figure out what had happened. He tried to hide his grief, but it was evident that he was hurting on the inside. Little did they know he was blaming himself for his wife's death.

"Mike is doing okay. They just wanted him to stay overnight for some more tests and observation. I'm going to pick him up later. Then I have to go to the funeral home and go over the arrangements."

"I'll go with you to help out with everything," Marcus said, patting him on the back.

"How about I go pick up Mike while y'all go handle the arrangements? He can just wait at my house until you get done. That way he won't have to be alone," Sasha suggested.

"Are you sure, Sasha?"

"Yeah, it's no problem. He's family, and we look out for each other."

"Thank you so much," Kevin replied.

"Well, let me go and get my phone and head to the hospital. If you need me for anything, just call. I have to make sure that Sahmeer is okay 'cause he was pissed when he heard about it on the news," Sasha said, giving Marcus a kiss and Kevin a hug.

After Sasha left, Marcus and Kevin were able to speak freely. They didn't want her to hear the real conversation.

"So do they have any leads on who did this yet?" Marcus asked.

"Not yet, but we came too far to go back to those ways. We wanted a better life for our families, and so far, we have done just that. We made it to the pros, and I'm not trying to mess that up. I hope you're not trying to do anything to jeopardize that either. Let's just let the authorities do their job on this one," Kevin replied, knowing that his best friend was ready to go to war.

"It's just crazy, man. She was family, so whoever did this needs to pay for this. I'm telling you now, if I catch them before the cops do, it's a wrap," he said, banging his fist into the palm of his other hand.

"I feel the same way, but we can't be in the public eye as heroes and vigilantes. Just chill for now."

"If that's what you want, bro, but if you change your mind, let me know. Our careers are almost over anyway. We're rich for life, but I do understand where you're coming from. We will need to get our sons ready for the league. Come on, let's go take care of the funeral arrangements," Marcus said.

"You think they will release her body this soon? I thought we would have to wait for them to finish the autopsy."

"We can just get everything else together and be ready when they do release her body," Marcus stated, finishing his drink.

~ ~ ~ ~

When Sasha arrived at the hospital, Mike was struggling to put his shirt on. She stood in the doorway admiring his muscular back. She felt the temperature rising between her legs.

"Need some help?" she asked, with a smile. That smile quickly vanished when he turned around to look at her. "Are you okay, Mike?"

She could see the hurt in his eyes. She really didn't know what to say or do because she had never lost someone so close before. Sasha grew up in an impoverished community, so she had seen a lot in her life, but to have it so close to home was a different story.

"I can't believe my mom is gone. Why did it have to happen to her? That should have been me that is about to be buried, not her," Mike said as tears ran down his cheeks.

"Don't say that, Mike. You have to be strong right now. They are going to find out who was responsible for the death of your mother. When they do, we will be right there to see them get the chair. Now let me help you get that shirt on."

As she helped him put his arm through the sleeve, Mike leaned in and kissed her on the cheek.

She looked into his eyes, and all she wanted to do at that moment was take his pain away. She gave him a peck on the lips, then his nose, his forehead, and then his lips once again. Even though it wasn't the right time or place for it, they both began to passionately kiss. Sasha stopped and moved back from his embrace.

"We can't do this here," she said. "What if someone comes in here and catches us?"

"That won't be a problem considering all the nurses are busy with the real patients. Give me a second," he stated, locking the door. "Now hop up on that bed and let me see something."

Sasha sat on the bed and opened her legs, exposing her neatly shaved mound. She stuck a finger inside, playing with her clit to get it nice and wet. Mike used his arm that wasn't in a sling, and pulled out his penis, stroking it to life. He climbed onto the bed and began to eat her pussy.

"Oh, baby, right there," Sasha moaned as he greedily sucked on her clit like it was a piece of candy.

He then got on top of her and entered her hot walls, sending her to an orgasm. The way he was moving in and out of her made her back arch and her toes curl.

"I love you, Mike," she whispered as she rolled onto her stomach, changing position so he could enter her from behind.

She continued to rub her clit while he fucked her in the ass. Mike admired Sasha's perfect body while filling the space between her legs. He rocked in and out of her, the whole time kissing the nape of her neck. He felt her body quiver as she reached another orgasm. With a few more deep strokes, he joined her in satisfaction. Sasha got up, fixing her skirt, while Mike tucked his penis back inside his pants. When they were dressed, they went to the nurse's station so he could sign out to go home.

"Did you really mean what you said when we were in the room?" he asked, getting into the car.

Sasha closed the door, then started the car up. She looked over to Mike and said one word, "Yes," as she pulled out into traffic.

CARLA WAS SITTING IN the waiting area of the doctor's office, waiting to be called. Her doctor had left a message on her voicemail, stating that she needed to speak to her. Ever since the rape, Carla had been on edge about everything. All of her tests had come back negative, even the HIV test, so she wondered what was wrong. She had an idea because her period hadn't come yet. She was two weeks late, so she was hoping she wasn't pregnant.

The doctor came out of her office and saw Carla sitting there reading a magazine. She said something to the receptionist and then walked over toward Carla.

"Good afternoon, Mrs. Wright. Would you please come with me to my office so we can talk?" she asked.

A sense of urgency suddenly came over Carla as she followed the doctor to the office. From the look on her face, Carla knew nothing good was going to come out of this. They entered the office and took a seat. The doctor searched through the pile of folders on her desk until she came across the one she was looking for.

"Well, Mrs. Wright, let's get right to it because I know you're wondering what this is all about. There was an error on your test that we took."

"What kind of error? Don't sugarcoat anything. Just tell me what the hell is going on," Carla replied anxiously.

Getting right to the point, the doctor started explaining what she was looking at in the folder.

"It seems your cells have taken a different turn. Your white cells are outnumbering your red cells. We retested your blood, and I'm very sorry, ma'am, but they came back positive," the doctor stated.

"Positive for what?"

"You tested positive for the HIV virus. We can retest if you like to be sure that we haven't made any mistakes."

"Damn right your gonna test me again. I can't have HIV. I want another test," Carla said hysterically.

"Okay, but there is something else. I hate to tell you this, but you're also pregnant."

That was the straw that broke the camel's back. Carla jumped out of her seat in a rage and started screaming all types of obscenities at the doctor, causing security to run into the office. The doctor told them that everything was okay, and they exited the office.

The tears began to flow down her face because she knew she had a bigger problem on her hands. She knew if she contracted the virus there was a 90 percent chance that the baby has it. She didn't know how she was going to explain this to her husband. This right here was going to put a dent into an already torn relationship.

"Why is this happening to me? What am I going to do? I can't bring this baby into the world like that. Please take the test over to make sure before I say anything to my husband," Carla pleaded.

"This type of stuff rarely happens, but let's go to the lab and run the test again. You need to start thinking about some important decisions, Mrs. Wright, just in case. I know this is hard to take in, but you will get through this. Just don't give up. I'm sure you have a great support system," the doctor said as they walked down the hall toward the lab.

Carla tried to take all of this in, but failed miserably. Her mind was blocked out with the fact that she might be dying from something that she tried all her life not to catch. As careful as she was, it only took one time to get caught up.

Two hours later, Carla walked out of the doctor's office in a daze. She had a bunch of pamphlets on how to cope with being HIV-positive. All the praying and hoping she did during the test came up unanswered. She cried so much that no more tears would come out.

"Ring, ring, ring."

She looked at her phone and saw that it was her husband. She was hesitant to answer it at first but did anyway.

"Hello."

"Where are you at? I thought you were going to make dinner tonight. When I got home, no one was here," he said, with a little sarcasm in his voice.

"I need to talk to you about something when I get there. Right now dinner is the last thing on my mind, so can you please stay there until I get home?"

"What's more important than me right now? I worked all day and can't even come home to a nice meal. Damn, you're probably out having fun with your friend, neglecting your responsibilities at home. If you're not here in the next forty-five minutes, I'm going out to eat," Morgan firmly stated.

"You are being such an asshole. I told you that I have something important to tell you, and all you're worried about is why I haven't made your fucking dinner. Well make your own dinner, because I'm not doing shit. I'll be there in twenty minutes. If you're there, I'll tell you what's going on. If not, oh well," she replied, then ended the call.

Morgan didn't know what had gotten into his wife, but he decided to stay in the house to see what her problem was. He called Symira and told her that he wouldn't be coming to the office tonight. They had planned to go to the movies to see Insidious 3, but it was going to have to wait.

When Carla walked into the house, Morgan could see that she had been crying. Not knowing what to say, he just waited for her to open up. Carla walked right past him and sat on the couch. Unable to hold back any longer, she broke down and told Morgan what was going on.

"I had to go see my doctor today, and she informed me that I'm pregnant," she said, looking at her husband to see what his reaction would be. To her surprise, there wasn't any.

"Are you sure?" was the only thing he said.

"What do you mean, am I sure? I'm fucking pregnant, and you want to know something else, I'm HIV-positive. Now what the hell am I supposed to do?" she said.

Morgan was speechless for the first time in his

life. He thought that he had heard her wrong until it kept playing over and over in his head.

"What do you mean you're HIV-positive and you're carrying my baby? How did this happen, Carla?"

"I'll tell you how it happened," she snapped. "I was raped, and you didn't even try to protect me. You never asked if I was okay or how I was feeling. All you're worried about is yourself and that bitch you're fucking. Don't worry. I'll be okay."

As Carla walked up the stairs, Morgan just watched in silence. He didn't know what to say, so he didn't say anything at all. Carla turned around and looked at him.

"Just so you know, the baby ain't yours." Then she continued to walk up the steps.

Morgan instantly got angry and ran up the steps behind her. When he reached the top, she slammed the door in his face.

"Open the door, Carla. What do you mean, it's not my baby? Well whose fucking baby is it then?" he said, pounding on the door trying to get into the room.

"Just go away and leave me alone. Don't you have some work to do or some bitch to screw? That's more important to you than family, so just go do it," Carla screamed through the door.

"Open this door before I break it . . ." he was saying until his cell phone went off. He looked down and saw that it was his secretary, so he walked away from the door and answered it. A couple of minutes later, Carla heard the front door slam. She looked out the bedroom window and saw his car pulling out of the driveway. She sat back down on the bed, with all types of thoughts going through her head. The most mysterious one was her thought of committing suicide. As she held the bottle of pills in her hand, she cried herself into a deep sleep.

~ ~ ~ ~

Kevin was sitting on the couch watching one of his old games when he heard a knock on the door. When he opened the door, there was a very attractive lady standing there.

"Yes, how can I help you?" he said, looking at 38DD breasts.

"Hello, I'm Detective Hill, and I'm the partner of Detective Davis. I just wanted to ask you a couple of follow-up questions."

Kevin looked at his watch wondering why she had come here alone after midnight to ask some follow-up questions. This was a strange time for another police interview, and what she wore said something else. She had on a button-up shirt with a casual skirt that was a little too short for an officer to be wearing.

"I don't have anything new for you yet, Detective," Kevin sighed. "Everything is still so blank for me. My wife never hurt anybody. Why would someone kill her?"

"That's what we are trying to find out sir. Well I guess that will be all for now," she said.

Kevin noticed that she couldn't take her eyes off of the bulge in his shorts.

"Sorry to bother you this late, Mr. Wright."

Kevin followed her toward the door. She was switching a little, which caused him to stare at her ass. He wanted to grab her skirt and lift it up so he could see what kind of panties she was wearing.

She hesitated as she reached for the knob on the door. Kevin could see in her face that she was here for something else. The tension in the room was electrifying, and his dick was trying to bust out of his shorts. She opened the door, slammed it, and then like an animal, she lunged at Kevin. He lifted

26

her up against the wall, and they kissed passionately. Kevin was grinding his dick on her pussy as
her skirt lifted up to her waist.

He carried her into his bedroom and dropped her
onto the bed. Detective Hill unbuttoned her shirt,
letting her breasts escape their captor.

"Holy fuck," he moaned, putting his mouth all
over each breast. He took his time, sucking on one,
then the other.

Next he started kissing all down her body, and
she knew where he was heading. The detective felt
like she was ready to cum just from his touch. She
was only thirty and had never had her pussy eaten
before. When he made it there, he pulled her panties
off and rubbed his hand between her legs. She was
dripping wet, and it turned her on even more,
knowing what was about to happen.

With his first lick, she screamed out. He buried
his face in her pussy and went to work. She never

felt anything so good in her life. His tongue dipping in and out, then he surprised her by shoving two of his fingers inside her pussy. That and him sucking on her clit gave her a sensation like no other. She had orgasms before, but nothing like the one she was experiencing at this moment. She screamed and bucked her hips as she came all in his mouth.

He moved up and kissed her hard on the mouth like he wanted her to taste her own cum. When he stood up, she pulled his shorts down, exposing the biggest dick she had ever seen. She stroked it for a minute, making it grow even longer, then she placed it in her mouth as far as it could go. She looked up at him while sucking his dick, to see his eyes rolling in the back of his head. That told her that she had him right where she wanted. He grabbed her hair and starting making her gag with each thrust. He was trying to make her take every inch of his shaft. Even though it hurt, she enjoyed it.

Kevin lifted her up and sat her down on top of him. She felt in between her legs for his dick and eased it inside of her. As she rotated her hips, Kevin began pumping faster and faster, trying to match her movements.

"This is what I needed right now. Damn, Michelle, I love you so much," he moaned.

Detective Hill heard what he said, and stopped. She got off of him, looking for her clothes.

"I didn't mean to say that," he said.

"I'm sorry, but I have to go. This is not right at all," she said, rushing for the door.

By the time he grabbed his robe and made his way downstairs, she was already closing the door.

Three

AKIYLAH WAS SITTING ON the couch watching *The Real World* when Sahmeer and Marcus walked in the door. Marcus nodded his head as he headed for the kitchen. Sahmeer sat next to her on the couch.

"Hey, baby, what you do all day?" he asked, giving her a kiss.

"Nothing, just cleaned up the house and the yard. I told your mom that I would cook dinner tonight."

"What are you going to make?"

"Maybe some Caribbean food or something. Is there anything in particular you want?" she asked.

"Whatever you make is cool with me. I'll be upstairs watching television if you need me," he said. He gave her a kiss on the forehead, then headed up the steps.

Akiylah walked into the kitchen and found Marcus sitting at the table drinking a beer. He didn't say anything, but just kept staring at her. She had been trying to avoid him for a few days now. Today her luck ran out because she had to be in the same room as him, even if it was only for a while.

"Come here for a minute so I can see what you have on under those sweats," he asked, with lust in his eyes.

She tried to ignore him, but he was persistent. He got up and walked up behind her. She squirmed out of his grasp.

"Me trying to prepare dinner for Sahmeer. Can you please leave me alone?" she said, moving toward the oven.

"I'll leave you alone when I want to. Now get the fuck over here right now."

Before she could move, Sahmeer walked in. He only heard the last part of what his father said.

"What's going on?" he asked.

"Nothing! I was just messing with my daughter-in-law. I'm about to pick your mom up from the shop. She had to leave her car there overnight. See you when I get back," he said, heading for the door.

After he left, Akiylah wanted to tell Sahmeer the truth, but she didn't know how. One thing she did know was that he would never touch her again. She would kill him first, even if it meant hurting the one she loved.

~ ~ ~ ~

Mike walked in the door and found his dad sitting in the dark. He put the light on, then walked over to where Kevin was sitting.

"Dad, are you okay?" he asked. He noticed that his dad had been crying. He sat next to him and placed his arm around him.

"We are going to be okay, Dad. You have to get yourself together for the funeral tomorrow."

"If I knew she was going to go like that, I would have told them to prepare two graves. I miss her so much," he replied, sobbing a little harder.

"Come on. Let's get you upstairs to bed. We have a long day ahead of us," Mike said, helping his father up the steps.

After he left his dad's room, he went back downstairs to watch television. The more he watched the show *Desperate Housewives*, the more he thought about Sasha. Terry Hatcher reminded him so much of her. He decided to call her to see what she was doing.

The phone rang four times before a yawning Sasha finally answered it.

"Hello."

"Hey, what are you doing sleeping at nine o'clock. It's still early, woman. Now get up," he joked.

"Mike, right now is not a good time. Marcus and Sahmeer are here," she whispered.

"I just wanted to see ya for a few minutes. Can you get away so we can have a little fun?"

"Listen," Sasha said, sitting up on her bed. "What we had was a little fling. We can't do this anymore because I don't want to get caught up and lose everything."

"I thought you said you loved me," he asked, confused.

"Mike, I do love you, but not in that way. We made a big mistake. Boundaries were crossed, and we can never take them back. All we can do now is cut it short before it gets too complicated," Sasha said.

"Complicated? It's already that way. I love you, and I want to be with you, Sasha. We can run away somewhere, just the two of us. No one has to know. We both have plenty of money, so we could live comfortably."

"Look, despite all the wrongdoings that I or my husband has done, I still love him, and he loves me. I'm not throwing that away, so I can't do that," she stated.

"So you just play with my emotions like this and now you're saying that it's over? Fuck it then, have it your way. Let's see who gets the last laugh," Mike said before ending the call.

"Hello, Mike, Mike," Sasha said, then realized he hung up on her. She wondered what he meant by that last statement. Her head started spinning out of control. She even contemplated not going to the funeral tomorrow. She had to go, though, because they were like family.

Mike threw his phone against the wall, watching it shatter into pieces. He was so mad that the only thing on his mind was revenge. He was going to make her pay for what she had done to him.

~ ~ ~ ~

"We are gathered here to celebrate the homecoming of our beloved sister, Michelle. We should not be sitting here mourning; we should be rejoicing. She has finally gone home to be with our father," the preacher said. Everyone started wiping their tears away and tried to smile, but it wasn't working. The church on 51st and Greenway was jam-packed. People were lined up outside to show their love for Kevin and his family. The police had blocked off all the streets surrounding the church. Only the people that were coming to the funeral were allowed inside the perimeter.

"Before we have the eulogy, we will now have a solo played by Michelle's cousin E.J., who came fr-

36

om Miami just to show his support to his family."

E.J. was sitting in the back row when they called him. As he walked down the aisle, everyone stared at him in amazement. Everyone that wasn't related to him was surprised to see him. They didn't know him, but they knew of him. He was a successful author, who moved out of Philly to Miami to try to start a new life for himself and his kids. His books, *Flipping Numbers* and *Lost and Turned Out* were best sellers. He walked up to the piano and sat down. Next he pulled the mic to him, adjusting it to his level. Then he began to play Michelle's favorite song: "Tender Kisses, blown away. Tender Kisses, gone tomorrow, gone today. Tender Kisses, bye baby, bye baby."

After he finished the song, he read the eulogy, then left the church to his awaiting limo parked outside. No one saw him after that. When the funeral was over and everyone had watched the casket being lowered into the ground, they went back to Kevin's house for the repast.

Marcus and Kevin were sitting in the kitchen talking when Morgan walked in. He greeted them with a half hug, then sat in one of the empty chairs.

"I need to talk to y'all about something. Someone caught me and my secretary committing adultery and has been extorting me for a while now. I gave him fifty grand, and now he still wants more. My wife has seen the tape, so now she knows. I hired this guy who specializes in getting rid of people, but since she knows now, I don't need him anymore."

"Wait a minute, you hired someone to kill your wife?" Marcus asked.

"No, no, I asked him to find the person extorting me, but he never did. I gave him some of the money, but I think he wants more. What should I do?"

They both looked at each other, then back to Morgan. They could see he was scared.

"Did he threaten you?" Kevin asked.

"Not yet, but I've been having a bad feeling lately, and since Carla lost the baby, my house hasn't been the same," Morgan said.

"Carla lost the baby...when?" Kevin questioned.

"It's a long story, but I guess I can give you the short version," he replied.

For the next half hour, the three men sat and talked. He told them everything, even the part about Carla having HIV. They couldn't believe what was going on in their peaceful community. Marcus gave him the only advice he could, and that was to get rid of this guy. It was going to be very difficult so they agreed to help him. The only problem was finding him.

Four

IT HAD BEEN A month since the death of Kevin's wife, and the police still didn't have a lead on the case. Even though they had ruled Kevin out of foul play, they still kept a watchful eye on him. Mike didn't go back to school, because he wanted to be close to his father. Sahmeer had decided to marry Akiylah next month. It would be a very small wedding. They wanted to wait a little longer because there was a lot of publicity being brought to their quiet, gated community. Reporters had been lurking around every day, waiting for that big break. Because Kevin was a star in the NBA, every sports channel had been airing a piece on him and his family.

Saleena had contacted Kevin and asked him to have dinner with her. They hadn't seen each other for a while, and he really wanted to see her, so he decided to go. When he arrived at the Italian restaurant, she was sitting there waiting. Saleena looked even more beautiful than the last time he saw her. She had on a black and gold Christian Dior strapless dress, with black and gold open-toed heels to match. Her hair flowed down her back, bringing out all her beauty.

"*Hola, hermoso, es bueno verte otra vez* (Hello, beautiful, it's good to see you again)," he said, kissing the back of her hand.

"*Gracias, Yo estaba Pensanda en ti mucho* (Thanks, I was thinking about you a lot)," she replied. She sat down and admired Kevin's handsome face.

He poured both of them a glass of wine, then passed her the glass. They toasted, then took a sip.

"*Yo estaba Pensanda en ti tabien* (I was thinking of you also)," he said.

"*Pues bien, después de la cena, tengo algo que mostrarte* (Well, after dinner, I have something to show you)," she stated seductively.

"You are too much," Kevin said, tired of speaking in Spanish. "The pleasure will be all mines."

She just smiled and took another sip of the wine. The waitress came over to take their order. They both ordered baked chicken, pasta, and a side of lasagna. Saleena's cell phone started ringing. When she saw who it was, she excused herself from the table and headed for the bathroom.

"Why are you calling me now? I told you I would come see you tomorrow," she said as soon as she entered the ladies' room.

"I need to meet with you ASAP. Something just came up, and it can't wait. We have to act on that other thing soon," the caller stated.

"Don't talk over the phone. I'll be there in thirty minutes," she said, ending the call.

Saleena powdered her nose, then returned to the table. Kevin noticed the change in her demeanor and asked, "Is everything okay?"

"*Lo siento, tengo que irme. Te llamaré mas tarde* (Sorry, I have to go. I will call you later)," she said, grabbing her shawl and heading for the door.

Kevin stood up and rushed after her. He caught up with her in the parking lot.

"What's wrong?"

"I have to go home. My mother is sick. I told you, I will call you later," she said, opening the car door.

"Okay, I hope she feels better," he said, showing a little sympathy.

When she left, Kevin paid the tab, then headed home.

~ ~ ~ ~

Morgan had just entered his office when Symira rushed in and closed the door.

"This guy is on the phone, and he wants to talk to you. I told him you weren't here, but he keeps calling every half hour on the hour. It might be that guy you hired," she whispered.

Morgan quickly walked over to the door, locked it, and then sat on top of his desk. He stared at the phone for a few seconds, held his finger up to his mouth signaling Symira to be quiet, then hit the speaker button.

"Hello, this is Morgan speaking. How can I help you?"

There was a brief silence; then the caller finally spoke with a low tone.

"You're a hard man to get in touch with. Why have you been ducking my calls?"

"The question is, why haven't you answered any of mine?" Morgan shot back, not the least bit intimidated.

"Because you never tried to contact me. That is about to change, though. I'll be there to see you real soon, and you better have the rest of my money."

"You're coming here?"

"Don't worry about it. Just have my money when I see you. Then and only then will our business be done with. You hired me for something; now you want to back out. It doesn't work like that," Kyle said.

"Fuck you," Morgan shouted. "I don't owe you anything. Who do you think you are, threatening me? I'm not giving you another dime. Do you hear that?"

"Okay, have it your way. See you when I see you. Oh yeah, by the way, how is your wife's health coming along?" Kyle asked.

"What the fuck you mean by—" But before he could finish, the phone had a dial tone. "This asshole is becoming a thorn in my side."

"What did he mean by that?" Symira asked.

Morgan just shook his head and said, "Nothing," while picking up the phone and dialing a number. "Give me a minute. I have to talk to someone in private."

"Listen, we are in this together. You can tell me what's going on," Symira stated, walking up to him trying to put her arms around his neck.

He pulled back from her, then stood up. She was stunned by the way he was acting.

"I said I need to take this call privately. I'll talk to you in a few minutes. Anything I have scheduled for today, reschedule it for later this week. Now excuse me," he replied, waving his hand for her to leave.

Symira stood there momentarily, then walked to the door. She turned around to say something, but he was already in conversation with whomever he had dialed. She exited his office and shut the door behind her.

"Where is Carla?" he asked the maid.

"She left a few minutes ago, sir. Should I deliver a message when she returns?"

"No, that's okay. I'll call her cell phone. Thank you," responded Morgan, hanging up before he got an answer.

He tried calling her phone three times, but it went straight to voicemail. He was wondering how the hell Kyle knew about his wife's health. He grabbed his jacket, then rushed out of the office. Symira was on the phone when he walked past her and got on the elevator.

"He just left," she said, before ending the call.

~ ~ ~ ~

Carla's stomach was starting to show just a little. She was really worried about the baby being born with the virus. It would affect everyone if that happened. She was just leaving Forever 21 at Christiana Mall when a group of girls sitting in the food court started following her. She was carrying two bags in one hand while drinking her coffee from Starbucks with the other.

As she exited the mall, she reached into her purse for her car keys. One of the girls rushed past her, grabbing for the bags. Carla tried to pull them back but was hit in the back of the head by one of the other girls. Two other girls rushed over and started hitting her in the stomach. Carla fell to the ground in a fetal position, trying to protect her unborn, but it wasn't helping. The girls kicked and punched on her until mall security rushed out to her rescue. They ran and jumped into the truck that was waiting, and sped off. Security was only able to get a partial of the license plate number.

Carla yelled out in pain, holding her stomach. An ambulance arrived within a few minutes after the incident. She was rushed to Christiana's emergency room to be treated.

"Slow down. I don't see anyone following us," one of the girls said, looking out the rear window.

The driver slowed down till she was doing the speed limit. She still checked the mirror periodically, making sure.

"She won't be having that baby now," the girl in the backseat stated.

"We made three hundred dollars for it. That was easy money for all of us. Let's get back to Philly now so we can give this truck back," the other girl said.

The four girls didn't even know the person that paid them to commit the crime. They only did it for the money. They each thought Carla was creeping around with one of the other girls' boyfriend. None of them even thought about the lie they were told, because they were young and dumb. If they had

49

gotten caught, they would have been doing time for someone else's treachery. They never thought about the cameras the mall's parking lot has. That night their faces were all over the news. This time they couldn't get away because people who knew them called the Philadelphia police department. All of them were arrested the next day.

A few hours later, some unknown individual bailed them out. The judge had given each one of them a $50,000 bail for aggravated assault. They only had to post 10 percent of that, which wasn't a problem.

~ ~ ~ ~

Morgan arrived at the hospital in no time. Carla was sitting up on the bed. She had just finished crying because she had lost another baby. When he saw the look on her face, he knew what had happened. He gave her a hug but wouldn't kiss her. It had been like that since he found out that she was

HIV-positive. His test came back negative, which was a relief to him.

"Why are you even here? It's obvious that you don't want me anymore," she said.

"What makes you think that? I'm here because you lost our baby and because I do care about you."

"No you don't. Just leave me alone. You can quit pretending and go back to that skank you've been having an affair with. I'm still filing for divorce," Carla said.

"Let's not forget that you also fucked that skank, and in our bedroom. So we are both guilty," he replied.

"Fuck you, Morgan. Get the hell out of here. I don't need you or your money. Y'all can have each other," she screamed.

Not wanting to create a scene, Morgan left. Besides, he was on his way to meet with one of his sources anyway. Carla sat back and thought about how she was going to get back at her husband for all the shit he had put her through. Most importantly, she wanted to get back at Symira.

Five

"OH MY GOD, BABY, that's my spot. Don't stop; it feels so good," Sasha moaned while lying in the back seat of her car. "Yes, you're about to make me cum."

Mike spread her pussy lips even wider as his tongue continued to massage her clit. He was definitely hitting her G-spot, and she enjoyed every minute of it. She started jerking and pulling away from his grasp, which meant she had reached her climax. Mike unzipped his jeans and pulled out his penis. He wanted to get his off now.

"Hurry up. We don't have that much time," she said, preparing for him to enter her moistened tunnel.

He wasted no time ramming himself inside her. She winced in pain from his thrust. He was acting like a maniac as he pounded away at her pussy.

"Ouch," she screamed. "You're hurting me. Slow down."

Mike acted like he was possessed as he ignored everything she said. They hadn't had sex in a month because she felt guilty about what they were doing. Mike saw her putting the trash into the garage and walked over to talk with her. He asked if they could do it one more time and he would leave her alone, so she agreed.

"Shut up and take this dick. You're my naughty little housewife. If this is my last time with you, then I'm going to enjoy it," he said, covering her mouth.

"Mmmmmmm," she said, trying to scream, but the sound was muffled by his hand.

At that moment, the garage door began to open. Mike saw it and bent down toward Sasha.

"Shhhh, someone is coming. Don't say anything," he said, but continued to pump in and out of her, trying to bust before they got caught.

The car pulled in right next to them, and Mike could see that it was Marcus. Sasha was petrified as they watched him exit his car. She wanted to scream for help, but she didn't want to get caught. She only had on a robe, with panties and no bra, so if Marcus saw her, he would know something was up. Her car was tinted, so there was no way he could see inside. He grabbed his gym bag out of the back seat, then headed inside the house. Once the door was shut, Mike continued pounding away as if it was the last piece of pussy on earth. Sasha started trying to push him off of her, but he was too strong.

"Get off of me, Mike," she screamed.

"Shut the fuck up," he replied, then slapped her. The blow shut her up momentarily. Then she started really screaming.

"Somebody help me, please," she said. "Please stop. I don't want to do this anymore."

Mike slapped her again and again and again, until she didn't scream any longer. Sasha had a busted lip, and her face was red. Once he realized what he had done, he stopped, fixed his clothes, then wiped her face with his shirt.

"I'm sorry, Sasha. I just got a little carried away. Please don't call the cops," he pleaded.

"You get away from me, Mike. I don't want to hear anything from you," Sasha stated. She fixed her robe and grabbed some tissues out of the glove compartment to wipe the tears from her face.

Mike didn't say anything before exiting the car and running out the door. Sasha took the makeup kit out that she kept in the car, then tried to cover up the bruises. She got out of the car, walked into the house, and tried to make it seem like she was in the bathroom. When she entered the bedroom, Marcus was just coming out of the shower.

"Hey, where were you?" he asked, drying himself off with the towel.

"Ugh, I was using the bathroom downstairs. I heard you come in, but I wasn't finished yet," she replied.

Marcus got up and gave her a hug and a kiss. He started rubbing his fingers across her nipples, bringing them to attention. As he went to stick his hand down her panties, she stepped back.

"Wait, baby, I have to take a quick shower. I just got finished doing a number two," she joked.

Marcus smiled at her. "Okay, but hurry up 'cause I'm feeling real horny right now, and I would like to make love to my beautiful wife. Oh yeah, and make sure you wash up good, 'cause I smell you."

Sasha faked a smile, then headed into the bathroom. She stayed in there so long that when she came out, he was asleep. Sasha was relieved, because her pussy was really sore from the beating it took a while ago. As she looked at herself in the mirror, tears began to fall. She couldn't help but think about what happened to her tonight. Her lip looked like it was swollen. It shocked her that Marcus didn't notice. She got into bed and fell asleep, with the hope that tomorrow would be a better day.

~ ~ ~ ~

Kyle was sitting at the table staring at a photo that he had received via certified mail. It was sent anonymously, so he didn't know who it came from. What he did know was it was his next target. Also inside the envelope was $10,000 cash. Who sent it didn't matter anymore. He continued to look at the picture because he thought he had met the person in it before. He just couldn't pinpoint where and when. Kyle finished his cup of coffee, then headed to the bathroom to take a shower.

After getting dressed, Kyle walked into his bedroom where his guest was still sleeping.

"Hey, get up. I have some business to take care of," he said, pulling the sheet off, revealing the caramel-complexioned female lying there. "Your money is on the nightstand. Get dressed. We're leaving in ten minutes."

"Why don't you just come back to bed and let me take care of you again? I promise it will be better," she said, spreading her legs.

As tempted as Kyle was, he passed on the offer. His business was more important than fucking the escort he had over. He had been fucking her for over a year now. He never used anybody else but her, even when she was fired from her job. Raquel had been fired about six months ago after testing positive for the HIV virus.

She had contracted it by shooting needles in her arm. Kyle had caught it from her after having unprotected sex. Now the two of them had been using the virus as a weapon. If she liked you, she would use a condom, but if you were a target, she would find a reason not to. There were times when she even went as far as poking a hole in the condom with her tongue ring while giving her johns or hits a blow job. Raquel and Kyle had formed a bond and had been unstoppable since.

"We don't have time for that. I have to hit this next target today," replied Kyle.

"So what do I have to do?"

"Nothing! This is a one-person mission, so I will be doing this by myself. I'll call you later when I'm done."

"Okay, make sure you do that," Raquel stated. She got dressed and was gone by the time Kyle came back from picking out a weapon from the other room.

Ready to go, he walked outside and hopped in the stolen car that he had taken the night before. He wanted to take care of this problem before tomorrow so he could leave the state. It was getting too complicated here, and he knew it was time to go.

As he drove onto the expressway, Kyle realized who the person was in the picture. He shook his head and smiled because he was about to see an old friend.

~ ~ ~ ~

"Do we have a lead on the Green case yet?" Capt. Turner inquired. "I'm getting a lot of shit from my bosses because this is a high-profile case."

"So far we are still at a standstill on this. All of the suspects alibis checked out. We're checking out a lead we just got, though. Hopefully we'll know something by tomorrow," Det. Hill stated.

"I hope so. Something needs to happen, and fast. I need someone in custody by next week. The reporters are everywhere," Capt. Turner said.

"Is that all you're worried about, sir? We have to do a thorough investigation to make sure we have the right person so it doesn't come back and bite us in the ass," Det. Davis replied.

"Just get it done," Capt. Turner retorted, then walked off, leaving the two detectives puzzled.

"I understand that this is a high-profile case, but he has to let us do our job. It's not like we're rookies," Det. Davis sighed.

Det. Hill just shook her head and got back to work. She had pulled up a lot of information on Kevin Green. Everything seemed to be in order, so she decided to look at all of their friends. One name in particular stood out to her. She decided to do as much digging without a warrant as she could. If everything wasn't up to par, she was going to try to get the warrants she needed.

"I need to speak with you. Could you come by the station, or would you like us to come to your house?" asked Det. Hill. She had made a call to talk with one of the people on their list.

After she hung up the phone, she looked over to her partner and gave him the thumbs-up. Det. Davis nodded, then made the call to Kevin.

"I hate to disturb you, Mr. Green, but I have a couple more questions for you if you don't mind."

"I'm close to the station. How about I drop by to answer them?" Kevin said.

"That would be perfect. I'll meet you at the front desk. Just tell them to page me when you get here," he replied.

"Will do," Kevin told him before ending the call.

"I will be talking to Kevin in a few minutes. Do you want to wait for me, or are you okay going by yourself?" Det. Davis asked his partner.

"I'm good, Pete. I'll meet you back here in a couple of hours," she smiled, retrieving her gun out of the drawer and holstering it.

Detective Davis watched his partner stroll out of the office, then retrieved some of his notes. He noticed that whoever shot Kevin's wife must have known them because there was no sign of forced entry. The first forty-eight hours were the most critical part of any homicide. It had been a little over two months, and they weren't any closer to solving this case like they thought they would be.

A few minutes later, Kevin walked into the station looking for Detective Davis. The front desk called him, and he came out a couple of minutes later. He escorted Kevin to one of the interview rooms so they could talk. Kevin remained calm because he knew they were only doing their job.

"This won't take long at all, Mr. Green," the Detective said, sitting down. He took out his pad to take some notes. "I know that we went over this already, but I forgot to ask you before. Did anyone else have a key to your house?"

"No one except me, my wife, and my son. We kept a spare key inside the flower pot. Only me and my wife knew about that," he responded.

"Okay! I'm just trying to narrow everything down. Your window and back side door were unlocked at the time, so whoever came in either knew y'all or knew the door was open."

"We live in a gated community. It's hard to get past the front gate. Security is very tight," Kevin said.

"I know, sir. We found a cut in the back gate. Whoever targeted your house knew exactly where they were going."

"So no one else's house was burglarized that night? Who would want to hurt my family?" he asked.

"To answer your questions, no, and I don't know. I was hoping you could tell me. Do you have any enemies?"

"Not that I know of. Look, I'm a basketball player. I travel from city to city meeting new people. I get along with everybody, and if I do have any enemies, I sure don't know about them." Kevin sighed. "All of this is just too much to bear for me and my son. We need to get some closure so we can move on."

"We're doing everything we can. I want you to go ahead on home, and as soon as we get something, you'll be the first to know," the detective said, walking Kevin back to the front.

After finishing up with Kevin, Detective Davis called his partner so they could meet up and compare interviews. They needed a suspect, and the case felt like it was starting to go cold, even though it'd only been a short while. She didn't know it yet, but Detective Hill finally had a lead in the case. Now she and her partner had to put it together.

~ ~ ~ ~

Kevin was on his way home, when his cell phone rang. He looked at the dashboard of his car and saw that it was Marcus.

"What's up, man?" he said, hitting the button on his steering wheel.

"Where are you? Allie and Katie want to meet up tonight. I told them I was gonna call you and set it up," Marcus blurted out.

"I had other plans, Marcus. You could have said something earlier. Me and Mike was gonna hang out. We haven't really had the chance because of everything that's been going on. Anyway, I don't think I'm ready to see somebody else yet. My wife will be turning in her grave," Kevin said.

"Come on, man. Look who you're talking to. You've been fucking other girls like you change your boxers. Even the day she was murdered, you were out with that Spanish chick. I hate to be so heartless, but grow a pair, man. You can chill with your son tomorrow. They are leaving for Cali in the morning, and they wanted to spend some time with us first."

"Okay, I guess it won't hurt. Knock on my door when you're ready," Kevin replied.

"I'll let them know. I'm headed home now to take a shower. I'll make up an excuse to tell Sasha.

She probably has something to do anyway. Later!" Marcus said, and then hung up.

Kevin headed home so he could get ready also. He needed to relieve some stress, and what better way to do so than with two beautiful girls.

~ ~ ~ ~

An hour and a half later, the two couples were sitting in Warm Daddies on Columbus Boulevard, enjoying the live band and eating soul food. Everyone came to South Philadelphia just to eat there. They had the best soul food in the area. Every Friday and Saturday there was a live band. The dress attire was casual, so Kevin and Marcus sported button ups with khakis. Allie and Katie had on strapless pencil dresses that showed off their curves.

"This food is delicious. I think I've found my new spot to eat at," Allie said, eating a fork full of cobbler.

"I've got something better that tastes good. Once you put it in your mouth, you'll never want to take it out." Marcus smirked.

"You're so nasty," Allie replied. "You can show it to me later if you play your cards right."

A smile came across his face at the thought of feeling her lips wrapped around his manhood. While Kevin and Katie had been sneaking around off and on, Marcus and Allie, on the other hand, had hardly seen each other. One or the other was always occupied. Truth be told, Allie really wanted Kevin. She had been spying on him since they all first met. When she and Katie talked about what he was like in bed, Allie's pussy would become moist. She even had dreams about the two of them having hot, wild sex. One time when he came to pick Katie up, she tried to get his attention by walking around in a wifebeater and skimpy shorts. As good as she looked in them, and knowing that he liked to fuck, he didn't pay her any attention. That only made her furious. She didn't like the fact that she was turned down, so she figured she'd give his best friend another chance. Tonight would be the first time she gave him some pussy.

"So where are we going after this?" Katie asked.

"I was thinking about stopping past Onyx. Then we could do whatever comes to mind," he suggested.

"Well let's go," Allie said, giving her friend a wink, then twirling her tongue at Marcus.

Marcus left a fifty-dollar tip along with the bill, for the beautiful waitress, then followed Kevin and the girls toward the door. They didn't have valet parking at the restaurant, but because of their celebrity status, Marcus and Kevin were able to park in the lot that was only used for handicap parking. They all hopped in Marcus's Bentley and headed down the street to Onyx.

When they pulled into the club, it was jam-packed. There were so many cars that they had to park outside the gates. It was a good thing they had valet parking there.

"Wow, this place is crowded tonight. I wonder what the special occasion is," Kevin said as they walked through the doors.

As if on cue, the DJ made an announcement, and about twenty girls walked onstage.

"Oh shit, a wet panty contest," Marcus blurted out.

Security and other workers started passing out super soakers to all the men and directed them toward the stage. Kevin and Marcus escorted the girls to the VIP Section, and they all watched the show.

A few of the dancers came up to them offering a lap dance, but only received tips. Allie and Katie were enjoying themselves, drinking bottle after bottle. They both were feeling tipsy and horny after the first forty-five minutes. As they were laughing and enjoying the scenery, a beautiful dancer approached them. Kevin couldn't believe how beautiful she was. She was milk chocolate and had long hair and a perfectly-shaped body. She looked like the spitting image of the actress Megan Good, but younger.

"Hello, my name is Diamond," she said, sitting between Marcus and Allie. "Would you and your girlfriend like a dance?"

He looked at Allie, and she nodded her head. A smile formed on his face. The three of them walked to the private room so they could be alone. Marcus paid the fee, then followed Diamond inside. Allie sat next to Marcus on the couch, while Diamond began to take off her bra and G-string.

The melody of R. Kelly's voice flowed through the speakers as Diamond did her dance:

"Temperature's rising and your body's yearning for me."

Just the sight of her twerking on Allie gave Marcus an erection. She started sliding up and down on Allie, making her dress rise up, exposing her panty-less mound.

Diamond did a split, then came back up riding Allie's crotch. As she did that, she started unbuckling Marcus's belt. She unsnapped his button, then pulled his zipper down. Next, she pulled out his rock-hard penis and started jerking him off as she continued to grind on Allie.

"Oh shit," Marcus moaned, with his eyes closed.

Diamond switched positions, placing her ass in the air toward Allie as she started giving Marcus a blow job. She placed two fingers inside Allie's pussy and started massaging her clit. This sent shock waves throughout Allie's body, bringing her to a climax.

Returning the favor, Allie stuck an index finger in Diamond's pussy while placing her thumb inside her anus. She simultaneously fingered both holes, causing Diamond to scream in pleasure. Marcus had had enough of the foreplay. He stood up and removed his pants.

"Come over here," he said to Allie, who stood up and bent over on the couch.

Marcus stood behind her, then spit on her asshole. She pulled out some lubricant that she kept in her purse, passing it to Diamond, who knew exactly what to do with it. She rubbed it all over Marcus's dick; then she spread Allie's ass cheeks apart while he positioned his penis at the hole. When he entered her, Allie began rotating her hips trying to find her rhythm.

Diamond sat on the couch in front of Allie, then put her legs on her shoulders. Allie knew exactly what she wanted, and gave it to her.

"You taste so good," Allie stated, coming up for air. "It smells like vanilla."

"Don't stop eating my pussy. You're doing so good that it's making me want to cum all in your mouth," Diamond moaned.

"Do it," Marcus growled, feeling himself about to ejaculate.

Soon as the words came out of his mouth, they all reached their climax at the same time.

"This was fun. We definitely have to do this again," Allie said, fixing her dress.

"Why don't y'all come through tomorrow night. Some of the girls are coming from K.O.D., and we're having a bikini boxing match," Diamond stated while counting all the money she just made.

"I don't know about that," Marcus said as he fixed himself up before heading back to the VIP booth where he had left Kevin and Katie.

"Here's my number. I make house calls," Diamond said before heading to the locker room to clean up. Allie stuffed the napkin with her number on it into her purse.

"I'll surely take you up on that offer," she said to herself.

"Damn, y'all sure look like y'all had fun," Katie said with a smile when they returned to the VIP booth.

Everyone laughed at the comment and poured some wine into their glasses. They enjoyed the rest of the night and got so drunk that none of them could drive home. They all ended up staying at the Hilton that night. Marcus got a suite on the top floor, with a swimming pool in it. The two couples fucked all night long without a care in the world. Diamond even joined the group. She brought two of her friends along. That was how they made it to the hotel, since no one could drive. She benefited from it in more ways than one.

The next morning when Marcus woke up, he had a splitting headache. He went into the bathroom to search for some Motrin. After washing his face and brushing his teeth, reality kicked in, and he knew he had fucked up. He wasn't supposed to be out all night. Sasha was going to be mad as hell. He figured he would just pick her up a gift with the hopes that she would forget about him not calling. When he walked out of the bathroom, Kevin was sitting up with the same headache.

"Damn, we messed up last night. You know we have to go to that meeting tonight to see if we're staying or being traded," Kevin said.

"I forgot about that," Marcus replied.

"Let's get out of here. I have to go home and get myself together," Kevin said. He put a thousand dollars on the nightstand for the girls, and the he and Marcus left without waking them up.

Six

SYMIRA AND MORGAN WERE in Las Vegas for the weekend. They had both told their partners that they had to stay in Washington because of the Democratic Convention. They gave them a story about supporting Clinton on her up-and-coming race for the presidency. The lie worked, which gave them some alone time.

"Let's go play some of the slots," Symira asked, rubbing Morgan's chest as they lay in bed.

"I don't feel like it right now. How about you give me some more of that head that I like," responded Morgan, trying to push her head down toward his waiting erection.

"Is that all you're thinking about right now?" she said, sitting up.

"Not really," he said. "I was thinking about giving you some head also."

He pulled her toward him as they kissed passionately. She grabbed the pillow and hit him with it. That started a pillow fight when he also grabbed one. The two played for a while before they both flopped down on the bed.

"Come on, babe, let's hit the slots for a couple of hours. I'll make it up to you when we get back," she said seductively.

Symira got off the bed and looked at him with pouting lips. He couldn't refuse that look if he tried.

"Okay, okay, but you owe me big when we come back," he said, slapping her on the ass. "Go ahead and get ready while I call my wife and check on her."

She gave him an evil eye before heading into the bathroom to freshen up. He wasn't really calling his wife. They hadn't said too much to each other since she lost the baby. Actually, that and the fact that she had the virus were driving them apart instead of bringing them closer.

After they both got ready, they headed downstairs to gamble for a couple of hours. Even though they eventually lost, they still had fun once they returned to their hotel room. The two shared a night of wild sex.

~ ~ ~ ~

Greg had just returned home from the bar. He was drunk and tired. He was only able to make it to his room before falling face first onto the bed.

"Fuck it. At least I made it this far," he slurred before passing out.

It was 3:15 a.m. when Greg woke up to a sensation that was all too familiar. He looked down at his wife's head moving up and down on his shaft. He was still too drunk to move. Everything seemed like a blur to him.

"Oh," was all he could say. He grabbed her head, moving it up and down as the feeling from her warm mouth took over.

She stood up, pushed him on his back, then straddled him, trying to be aggressive. Greg wondered what has gotten into his wife because she never acted this way. Whatever, it was, he was enjoying it. She leaned down to kiss him, but he flipped her over instead. With force, he ripped her shirt off, exposing her already hard nipples, then removed the shorts she was wearing.

He hungrily sucked on her nipples, alternating between them, teasing each one with his tongue. She moaned in delight as she watched his head venture between her quivering thighs. Greg made love to her with his salacious tongue until she drenched his face with her juices. He was so turned on by now that he decided to give her another orgasm. He mounted her gently, entering her hot walls with precision. She felt every inch of him with each lingering stroke. He moved in and out sensually slow.

With every thrust, she felt waves of currents throughout her entire body. He built up the momentum until he knew she was about to reach her peak, then slowed down his pace, causing her to lose composure. She started moving back and forth, forcing him to continue. He happily obliged. Her body jerked as she reached her second orgasm. Bringing her body to ecstasy forced him to also shoot his load.

"Damn, baby, that pussy is lethal," he said, out of breath. He rolled over on one side of the bed, trying to find the light switch.

She didn't even respond to his comment. When he turned on the light, he only got a glimpse of her walking out of the room. She closed the door behind her.

"Symira, where are you going? Bring me something to drink before you come back in here," he hollered out.

She smiled as she slid into her shorts and slipped on one of his shirts, before heading out the door. As she got into her car and pulled off, she thought about her little sexcapade she just had, and got wet all over again. She hadn't thought it would be that good.

"If only you knew how lethal," she said to no one in particular as she pulled out into traffic with a smirk on her face.

A few minutes went by, and Symira still hadn't come back into the room. Greg got up and went downstairs looking for her. He checked in the kitchen, she wasn't there. When he walked into the living room, he noticed a note on the door. He grabbed it and read the message.

Hey,

Sorry I had to leave so fast. You

were great. Maybe I'll give you some

more one day. TTYL!!

Greg looked at the note and wondered who the hell was just in his bedroom. If he wasn't so drunk, he would have realized it wasn't his wife he was with. He needed another drink right now to clear his head. He wasn't as drunk anymore, so he had his sense of awareness back. After checking the locks on the door, pouring a drink, and cutting off the lights, he went back upstairs to his room to relax. He had to admit, whoever he was with had some good pussy.

~ ~ ~ ~

Sasha was on her way home from the hairdresser when she decided to stop and pick up a pizza for her and the family. The pizza shop was a little crowded when she walked in, so she turned around to leave. Before she walked out the door, someone tapped her on the shoulder.

"Excuse me, miss, don't I know you from somewhere?" the man asked.

Sasha stared at him momentarily, trying to figure out who he was. After a couple of seconds, she remembered.

"The delivery guy?" she said.

"Yes! I haven't delivered to you in a while. What, you don't like our food anymore?" he joked.

Sasha just smiled at the comment. "No, we just been doing other things."

"Well it's nice to see you again. Did you want to order?" he said.

"It's too crowded, and I'm kinda in a rush," Sasha replied. She could feel herself getting a little hot from staring at his strong arms fighting their way out of the short sleeve shirt he was wearing.

"Come on in. I'll take your order myself."

She followed him inside to the counter so she could get her food and hurry home. If no one was at her house, she would have told him to deliver it to her, but she had talked to Marcus and Sahmeer earlier. She placed her order, and to her surprise, he had it ready in no time. She paid for it plus gave him a tip, then headed home.

"Nice seeing you again. You can always call, and I will come to you," he yelled out as she rushed out the door.

"I sure will," she thought, getting into her car. She made it home in ten minutes. When she pulled up, she noticed that Marcus's car was gone. She grabbed the buffalo wings and two boxes of pizza and went inside.

"Marcus, Sahmeer, dinner is here," she yelled up the steps. She got no answer. She sat the food on the table, then went to see where they were.

As she walked up the steps, she could hear the shower running. She checked her room, no sign of Marcus. She went into Sahmeer's room. Same result: empty. She heard singing coming from the bathroom, so she knocked on the door.

"Yes, me almost done," Akiylah said.

"It's just me, Akilyah. Where did the boys go?" she asked.

"You can come in," she said. "They went to the gym. They thought you would be a while."

Sasha opened the door and saw Akiylah washing the soap off her body. She continued to stare at her in awe. Her body was beautiful. Sasha unsuspectedly felt a tingle in her panties. She never really looked at her daughter-in-law in that way until now. Akiylah's curves were perfect, and the water running down her body had Sasha in a trance. She sat on the toilet and talked to Akiylah while enjoying the view.

"I told them I was coming with food. They shouldn't have left. How long have they been gone?"

"About fifteen minutes. Me will eat with you as soon as me finished," she said in her Caribbean accent. "Can you wash me back, Mrs. Sasha?"

"Sure," Sasha replied as she walked over to the shower. She opened the glass door and took the sponge from Akiylah. Sasha rubbed her back gently with the sponge. Akiylah's breath became shallow as she felt Sasha's soft hands caress her back. Sasha started at the top and rubbed the soap lower and lower until she reached Akiylah's ass. Sasha dropped the sponge and began to rub her hands all over Akiylah's back.

The feeling of Sasha's hands on her body made Akiylah's nipples hard. A sensation of pleasure went off in her body like no other. Sasha's hands traveled south, and she ended up massaging her caramel mounds.

"Mrs. Sasha, what are you doing?" Akiylah whispered as she felt her pussy start to throb.

"Relax, I'm loosening you up," Sasha replied sweetly.

Sasha removed the sun dress she was wearing and got all the way inside the shower, shutting the door behind her. Her hands moved around the front of Akiylah's body and caressed her breasts. Her nipples were on point, and Sasha pinched them gently, causing tingles to shoot up and down Akiylah's spine.

"You want me to stop?" Sasha asked.

"No," Akiylah admitted.

Sasha turned her around, and they stood breast to breast momentarily. Then they began kissing as the water sprayed their bodies. Sasha's mouth found Akiylah's nipples, and she sucked on them slowly, rolling her tongue over her breasts. Sasha put her hand in between Akiylah's legs and felt that her clitoris was hard, and began to grind her own against it.

"Damn, Sasha, what are you doing to me body?" Akiylah moaned in a pleasure-filled tone.

That was the first time she ever called Sasha by her first name instead of saying "Mrs." Sasha didn't respond. Instead, she simply got on her knees and tantalized Akiylah's pussy with her tongue until Akiylah had an explosive orgasm. They both rinsed off and got out of the shower, neither saying a word about what had just happened.

Sasha grabbed her clothes off the floor, then went to her room to get dressed before the boys came back.

Akiylah did the same, but she couldn't help but smile as she pictured Sasha's mouth eating her pussy. She needed something hard now to take the edge off, and she knew exactly who could do it.

By the time Marcus and Sahmeer returned from the gym, the food was cold. Sasha and Akiylah had already eaten and were watching a movie.

"Sorry. We thought you were going to be out longer," Marcus stated, giving Sasha a kiss on the cheek.

"Whatever. Y'all can go warm your own food up. I'm going to bed," Sasha replied, getting up and heading upstairs.

"Wait for me," Marcus said, leaving Sahmeer and his wife downstairs.

"Me will warm you food up," Akiylah said, heading into the kitchen. She knew Sahmeer would be watching, so she twisted her hips a little extra for him to see.

Sahmeer walked into the kitchen to find Akiylah sitting on the table. Her skirt was so short you could

92

see her black lace panties underneath. She leaned back and spread her legs seductively. She stuck one finger in her pussy and then lifted it up to his lips.

"Come taste me," she said as she licked her lips.

He licked her wetness off of her finger as he ground his hardness against her body.

"Hmmm," he moaned as he began to nibble gently on her neck.

Sahmeer's hands sent electricity up her spine. He knelt down on one knee and slipped his tongue into her pussy, twirling it in circles inside of her. She moaned so loudly that she was sure his parents heard her. This was one of the best head games she had ever had.

Sahmeer inserted two fingers into her opening as his tongue played with her clitoris. She moved her hips like a dancer, winding like a Jamaican while pressing her vagina against his mouth. It felt so good that she couldn't help but grind back with aggression. Sahmeer put his hands underneath her skirt until both of them gripped her ass cheeks. He massaged them as he helped her grind her pussy on his tongue. He reached down with one hand and started stroking himself to bring his man to full attention.

Akiylah looked down and watching him pleasing himself. She quickly pulled him up and inserted his dick into her vagina, not wanting him to bust before she felt him inside her. The satisfied look on his face brought her to climax, and she felt herself cumming all over him. Seconds later, he grunted loudly as he also erupted inside her. Akiylah looked toward the door and found Marcus watching with his dick in his hand, jerking off.

"Oh my God," she said, startled.

Marcus snuck away before Sahmeer turned around to see what scared her.

"What's wrong?" he said, fixing his pants.

"Nothing. I thought I saw a mouse," she lied. "We need to get our own place soon."

"We will next month. I already found one for us. My dad is going to sign for it when the family leaves for Florida," he said, giving her a hug.

She couldn't wait to get out of there. She didn't know how much longer she could go without saying something. Especially now that she had fucked both of his parents.

Seven

KEVIN AND MARCUS WERE leaving from the meeting they had with their coach. They found out that they weren't going to be traded and would be spending what might be their last year with the same team.

"Well, I think we should go out with a monster year 'cause I'm quite sure we won't be getting any time next year," Marcus said as they got into the car.

"That's if we get any playing time this year. Look at all the new guys they signed. Our time is definitely up after this. We will definitely see a drop in minutes and will have to educate the rookies to carry the torch," Kevin said.

"I don't know about you, but I'm going for the scoring title this season," Marcus boasted.

"Not if I can get it. You know I put the points up on that team," Kevin chuckled.

"We'll see about that."

They both laughed as they headed home. When Marcus stopped at Kevin's house, Mike and Sahmeer were playing a game of one-on-one. Both men sat there admiring their sons' skills.

"Look at our future right there. They will continue our legacy for the next twenty years," Kevin stated.

"I sure hope so. They got skills too," Marcus replied. "Let's go show them how it's really done."

Kevin and Marcus got out of the car and walked over to the court where their boys were playing.

"What's up, boys? Y'all ready for a rematch?" Marcus asked them.

"Come on, old timers, let's see what you got left in those tanks," Mike chuckled, passing them the ball. "Check it up."

The four men played for the next hour, before they all got tired. Marcus and Kevin lost to their sons 34–18. That's when they knew they had raised some talented sons and hoped that they both got into the NBA one day.

"I'm going to take a shower. I'll catch y'all later," Marcus said, walking toward the house.

"I'll be back in a few, Dad. Me and Mike are going to pick up something to wear to the party tonight," Sahmeer said.

Mike went home and grabbed his car keys, and the two boys left for the mall. As Marcus walked into the house, he smelled an all-too-familiar fragrance coming from the kitchen. He walked into the kitchen and found Akiylah over the stove cooking a Caribbean dish. The smell was very enticing to the nose.

"That smells good," he said, startling Akiylah. "You mind if I have a taste?"

"Sure, me should be finished in a couple of minutes," she said, trying to be nice. Deep down inside she couldn't stand being alone with him in the same room.

"Did Sasha come back yet?" he asked as he walked over to where she was standing.

"No," Akiylah replied, trying to give them some space.

She had on a pair of sweatpants with the word "Juicy" on the ass. That made Marcus stare momentarily as he tried to find an excuse to get closer to her. She moved over to the sink to wash the used dishes, and Marcus closed the space between them, wrapping his arms around her.

"I was talking about tasting you, not the food," Marcus said, trying to kiss her neck.

Akiylah tried to break free from his grasp as he fondled her body. He was persistent and kept a hold on her so she couldn't run anywhere.

"Please, me don't want to do that," she complained. That only made Marcus want her more.

"What did I tell you I would do if you keep refusing me, huh?" he said, trying to pull her titties out from the shirt she was wearing.

"Why don't you tell me what you told her?" a voice said, causing both of them to look up.

Standing in the doorway was Sahmeer. He and Mike had turned around because he had forgotten his wallet. He heard the commotion coming from the kitchen and went to see what was going on.

"Son, what are you doing here?" Marcus said, stepping away from Akiylah. She fixed herself and wiped the tears from her face.

"Dad, what were you just doing to my wife? No, better yet, why the hell did you just have your hands on her?"

Marcus was stunned. He didn't know what to say or do at this point.

"She was trying to come on to me. This has been going on for a while now. I told her I was going to tell you if she didn't stop," Marcus lied.

"It seems like it was the other way around," Sahmeer stated, walking toward Marcus.

"He tried to rape me," Akiylah blurted out, crying. She was hoping that she didn't have to say anything about the other times.

"Stop lying, bitch, for I—" That was all Marcus could get out before Sahmeer punched him in the face, sending him flying into the refrigerator. The next blow crumpled him to the ground.

The look on his face said he wanted to kill his dad. The reason he didn't was because Akiylah started screaming. He picked up the iron pan from the stove and raised it in the air.

"Sahmeer, stop, please! Me don't want you to go to jail," Akiylah screamed with pleading eyes.

Just then, Mike walked in and was able to grab Sahmeer's hand before he did something he would have regretted for the rest of his life. Sahmeer's eyes were so red that if he blinked the wrong way, fire might start shooting out.

"Go pack your stuff. We are leaving right now," Sahmeer demanded, looking at Akiylah.

She rushed out of the kitchen and headed upstairs to do as she was told.

"What the hell just happened?" Mike said, looking at his friend, then at Marcus.

Mike was dumbfounded. He didn't know what to say about the news he had just received. He looked at Marcus for an explanation, but didn't get one, which led him to believe that it was true.

"Sahmeer, let me explain," Marcus said, trying to get up from the ground.

"I don't want to hear it. We are leaving, and you will never have to worry about us again," Sahmeer firmly stated, leaving his dad there wiping blood from his mouth. Sahmeer walked back into the kitchen, looked at his father, and said, "And you don't have to worry about being a grandfather either."

That statement shocked both Marcus and Mike. They didn't know that Akiylah was pregnant. In fact, no one did. Sahmeer was going to tell everybody at his mom's party tonight. That was going to be their birthday present to Sasha, letting her know that she would soon be a grandmother. Now there was a chance that she and Marcus wouldn't even see their son's family anymore. To add even more drama to the situation, Akiylah didn't know if the baby was Marcus's or Sahmeer's. She didn't want to say anything about it right now. She actually was going to wait until the baby was born, then try to get a DNA test without them even knowing.

~ ~ ~ ~

Sasha arrived home furious at the news she received a few minutes ago. When she walked in the door, Marcus was sitting on the couch holding an ice pack to his jaw. She walked over to him and smacked it out of his hand.

"You need to pack your shit and leave right now. Don't you say a word 'cause I don't want to hear it," she said. "How could you do this to our family? You just don't care about anybody but yourself, do you?"

She didn't even give him time to respond. She ran up the stairs and began throwing his stuff down to him. Marcus stood at the bottom of the stairs, with a blank look on his face.

"Baby, you got it all wrong," he managed to say.

"I got it all wrong?" she said, walking down the steps. "I got it all wrong? My son and his wife call

104

me crying, telling me how you tried to sexually assault her, but I got it all wrong, huh? I don't care who you go out there sticking your little thing in, but why would you do that to your own son?"

Marcus didn't even say anything because he already felt like the scum of the earth. Her talking only intensified the guilt he was feeling. He just walked out the door without another word. Sasha also felt guilty because she did the same thing not so long ago. The only difference was, *they* both enjoyed every second of it.

She gathered up the stuff she threw down the steps, and sat it outside. While she was doing that, Mike walked over to where she was standing.

"Sasha, I just want to apologize for what happened between us, and I hope you don't hate me," he said sincerely.

She could tell by his demeanor that he was sorry. She didn't want to be mad at him anymore, but she knew they couldn't cross those boundaries again, and that was for sure.

"You're forgiven, Mike, but that is where it ends, okay? You can visit my son all you want. I just don't want anything to do with you as far as we are concerned, okay?"

He nodded his head, then walked away. She stood there, watching until he walked inside the house. Sasha finished putting Marcus's clothes outside, then went back inside to call everyone and let them know that the party was canceled tonight. There was no way she was having a party with all the drama that had unfolded in that little bit of time. What started off as a promising day, ended up being one of the worst days of her life. All she could do now was hope that her son didn't find out about her sins, because he would hate both of his parents. Her secret went deeper than the affair she had with

Akiylah. That was a part of her life that would ruin their family for sure.

Eight

KYLE HAD BEEN WATCHING his target closely for the last few days. He figured tonight was the time to eliminate his contract so he could move on to other things. He was sitting on the roof across the street from city hall, watching the fiasco going on in the streets. Protestors and supporters were shouting and holding up signs. Police officers and federal agents were everywhere. The whole perimeter was blocked off, but that wasn't going to stop Kyle from handling his business. He started putting his .30-30 rifle together with precision. After everything was in place, he loaded one round into the chamber, then looked through the scope to focus on his target.

"We're live at city hall, where the governor is about to make his speech about the budget for the schools in Philadelphia. The mayor will also speak today on the tax increase in our city," the reporter said to all the viewers watching the Channel 6 News.

Everyone was gathered downtown to see firsthand what the government plans were. They wanted to raise taxes on sodas to pay for funding in other areas. Parents and children wanted to see what schools would be closing this coming school year, while others waited to hear if marijuana was going to be legal.

People started cheering when they saw a fleet of limos in the distance getting closer and closer. It was the governor's vehicles approaching. Police officers started forming barricades, while the secret service did their job of making sure the area was safe. The limo carrying the governor pulled up in front of the podium, and cameras began flashing from everywhere. Video feed started rolling, and people started clapping. The door opened, and the first person to step out was Morgan. This was one of the perks of being the governor's assistant. The governor and his wife were the next to exit the vehicle. They waved as they headed to the stage where the governor would make his speech. Morgan loved being in the limelight. He felt like it was his calling. He stood next to the governor as he greeted the mayor of Philadelphia, then stood on the stage waiting to be introduced to the public.

Kyle sat on the roof watching and waiting patiently for his moment to strike. He was on his eighteenth cigarette and was about to smoke another one. He was sweating profusely from anticipation and the heat that was beating down on him.

He lifted the rifle up on the ledge. The time had come for him to get his mark. He looked through the scope, aiming at his target, finger on the trigger, ready to squeeze.

~ ~ ~ ~

Detectives Hill and Davis had just arrived and were waiting to see if any of the budgets had anything to do with the Philadelphia police department. They had heard rumors that the mayor wanted to start a special unit that would specialize in only guns and ammo. If so, they wanted to be a part of that unit. Homicide was getting boring for them.

"I hope the rumors are true about that special unit," Det. Hill said to her partner, sipping on her coffee.

"Me too, 'cause I'm trying to be on top of that list. There ain't too many people on the force with our qualifications and seniority," he replied.

"Yeah, but the higher ups don't look at it that way. Maybe if we hurry up and solve that Green case, we'll get the break we've been waiting for," she stated.

"That's true. We will get back at it tomorrow, but for now, let's see what our bosses have to say." He smirked.

They showed the officers guarding the perimeter their credentials, then proceeded toward the stage to get front-row seats at the event.

"Look at the turnout," Det. Hill mentioned, looking at all the spectators in attendance. "I didn't know this many people cared about hearing from the governor."

"They don't; they just want to know what's going on with the taxes and schools. Read the signs," he said as they took their seats.

~ ~ ~ ~

"Now, without further ado, I present to you our governor of Pennsylvania, Governor C.," the announcer stated. There were some cheers as well as some boos as he approached the mic.

"Thank you city of Philadelphia and everyone else watching around the world," he started off. Morgan was standing by his side the whole time as he began his speech.

Kyle's finger was on the trigger, and he slowly pulled back, making sure he had a clear sight of his target. The shot was a direct hit, and people started scrambling as the body dropped.

He quickly gathered up and ran for the shaft door to make his escape. He ran down the steps and into the garage, straight for the car he had stolen. He threw the gun in the backseat and hopped in the driver's seat.

~ ~ ~ ~

"Shots fired, shots fired. We have one person down and the gunman somewhere in the area," Det. Davis shouted over his radio.

He and his partner already had their guns out and were running toward the area where the shot came from. As they got close to the building, they noticed a car speeding out of the parking garage. They immediately opened fire on the vehicle. Detective Hill aimed for the tires and hit the right rear one, causing the car to spin out of control. Detective Davis also hit the back window, shattering the glass. They approached the car with caution, but before they got within twenty feet, the driver opened fire.

"Requesting backup, shots fired," she shouted into the radio as they took cover.

Kyle had managed to crash into a pole without getting hurt. He quickly pulled his .40 cal. out and started returning fire. He knew it was a matter of time before hundreds of cops would be there. As he tried to make a run for it, he caught two bullets in his back and fell on his face. All this time he had been doing hits, he never thought he would get caught like this.

"Suspect is down. I repeat, suspect is down," Det. Hill spoke through the radio as they approached the man on the ground.

"Drop your weapon," Det. Davis shouted.

Kyle couldn't move from the pain in his chest. His gun was only a couple of feet away. If he was going to die, he was taking one of them with him. Before he could get to it, Det. Davis was on him.

"Don't you even think about it," he said, aiming at his head. Det. Hill picked the gun up and covered her partner while he cuffed the suspect.

"We need a bus. Suspect is still alive. I repeat, we need a bus; suspect is still alive," she yelled over the radio.

The ambulance came and began working on Kyle. They wanted him alive so they could find out what made him do what he did.

"Get the car, and I'll ride with the suspect," Det. Davis told his partner. He jumped into the ambulance as they hit the sirens and headed for Jefferson Hospital.

"Who hired you to do that, and I'll make sure you live," Det. Davis whispered in Kyle's ear.

He wouldn't say anything, so Det. Davis squeezed the IV, causing air to go into his veins. Kyle felt the pain and started trying to get free, but the handcuffs held him to the gurney. "I said, tell me who hired you."

"Detective, you can't do that to the patient. I will report you if you don't stop," the paramedic protested.

"You stay the hell out of this. He is a prime suspect in a shooting, and he is gonna tell me who he works for," Det. Davis replied.

He squeezed on the IV once again. This time it sent Kyle into shock. He started shaking uncontrollably, then flatlined. The paramedic watched in horror as the detective was trying to kill his patient.

The driver pulled over and ran to the back. She got in and shut the door.

"I don't care who you think you are, but I will not let you kill a patient on my watch. Now you get out of the way and let us do our job," she said angrily.

They started CPR and shocked Kyle until they had a pulse again. Det. Davis didn't want to kill the suspect; he just thought he would get some information out of him. As they pulled into the emergency area, he noticed a key sticking out of Kyle's pocket and grabbed it. It was a motel key to the Red Roof Inn. If there was a clue, he was hoping it would be there. His partner pulled up, and Det. Davis hopped in the car.

"Did you find anything in his car?" Det. Davis asked as soon as he shut the door.

"Not really! The car was stolen, and the plates were fictitious, but I did get a receipt from a credit card with the name Raquel Jackson on it. That's not the name of the car owner. Whoever she is was staying at a motel . . ."

"The Red Roof Inn," he said, beating her to it.

"How did you know that?" she asked, with a smile. He held the room key up for her to see. "I should have known. So I guess that's where we are headed first."

He nodded as she hit the sirens, trying to get there in a hurry. They hoped that this Raquel person would still be there and could shed some light on this chain of events.

"We have to hurry, just in case the feds try to take over the case," Det. Davis said, watching traffic as Det. Hill sped through light after light.

They reached the motel twenty minutes later. They walked up to the room and knocked on the door. No one answered after the third time, so Det.

Davis used the key card. Pulling their weapons, they entered with caution.

"Anyone here? This is the police," he shouted. They checked each area of the room.

"Clear," she said.

"Clear in here also," he told his partner.

They searched the whole room but didn't find anything useful. The place was clean. As they were leaving, a woman was walking their way. As soon as she saw them, she knew they were cops and took off running.

"Freeze, police," Det. Hill shouted as they gave chase.

Raquel only made it to her car before they caught her. Det. Hill placed the handcuffs on her as Det. Davis read her her rights.

"Sit here and don't move," Det. Davis told her. "Why did you try to run away?"

Raquel didn't say a word. She just stared at the cops like they were trash. Det. Davis searched her car and discovered two DVDs and a recorder. He also found a loaded handgun under the driver side seat.

"Well, I guess you'll be coming with us," Det. Hill said smiling at the lady.

~ ~ ~ ~

The two detectives, the ADA, and the captain sat in a room watching the DVDs. They couldn't believe their eyes at what they were seeing. It showed two people, that they recognized as the governor's assistant and his secretary, engaging in lewd acts inside a hotel room. The next one showed them in his office. They stopped the video and looked at each other, shaking their heads.

"So what does this have to do with the shooting earlier?" Captain Kimenski asked.

"This could be part of it," Det. Hill said, pressing play on the recorder in her hand:

"I want this harassment to stop before it costs me everything. I want you to find the bastard and put him on ice."

"You know what you're asking me to do, right?"

"I know exactly what I'm asking --."

She stopped the recorder so everyone could take in what they just heard.

"So that's the guy at the hospital and the governor's assistant conspiring to commit murder, but who are they trying to kill?" the ADA asked.

"That's the million-dollar question, and only the three of them can answer unless we have someone else," Captain Kimenski said. "Hill, you question the girl. Davis, go back to the hospital and question that shooter. Don't come to my office without an answer."

"They don't think he's gonna make it, Captain," Det. Davis told her.

"Well I guess you better make sure he gives you his dying declaration then, Detective," she replied, then headed out of the room.

"Good cop, bad cop?" Detective Hill asked her partner as they headed toward the interview room.

"I'll be the bad cop for this one," he smiled.

"As usual," she said as they walked into the room. They interrogated Raquel for two hours before she finally broke down and told them everything they needed to know. She even told them how she and Kyle had given their victims the virus to a slow death. Most importantly, they had a name and the reason why he had hired them to do it. Det. Davis felt like this case was an open and shut one, and they solved it without the help of the feds.

~ ~ ~ ~

Carla was sitting in the house watching *General Hospital*, her favorite soap opera, when a breaking news bulletin shot across the screen, interrupting it. She got up and went into the kitchen to refill her cup of coffee. When she walked back in, the shooting at city hall was on. She watched as they talked about the governor being shot. She saw her husband talking to the cops, and a sigh of relief came over her.

Just as she was about to take a sip of her coffee, the picture of the shooter was displayed. She spit the coffee out, as she remembered his face. It was a face she would never forget.

"That's him," she said to herself. She quickly reached for the phone and called her husband.

It rang several times before going straight to voicemail. She tried again with the same results. She needed to talk to him, so she grabbed her purse and ran out the door. She was shaking at the thought of what that monster did to her. Carla hit the alarm to her car and pressed the button to the garage door as she started the engine and rushed off to city hall. As she drove, she kept calling her husband, with no answer.

She called the office phone, and Symira answered after the third ring.

"Hello, how may I direct your call?" she said.

"Symira, where is Morgan? It is very important that I speak with him," she stated.

Usually, Symira would have made up an excuse, but this time she could hear the sense of urgency in Carla's voice. That told her that something was really wrong.

"He is at the hospital with everyone else, waiting to hear the status of the governor. Is everything okay?" she asked, concerned.

"I just need to speak with my husband. If you talk to him, tell him that I'm on my way to the hospital and that it's an emergency," she told her before ending the call.

Symira didn't even get a chance to respond before she heard a dial tone. Since she was rude, she forgot about the whole conversation that they just had.

"I'm not telling him shit," she said, sucking her teeth.

Carla was driving recklessly as she headed to the emergency room. Then it hit her: she didn't even know which one they were at. She turned on the radio, switching to KYW News Radio, and just like clockwork, they were talking about it. She headed straight for the trauma unit at the University of Pennsylvania.

When she arrived, everything was blocked off, and no one could get through unless they were in an emergency vehicle. Since Morgan was her husband, a lot of the secret service there knew her. She called out to one of them, and they immediately let her pass. It seemed like every law enforcement agency was there. She quickly jumped out of the car and searched for Morgan.

She found him talking to a group of men and rushed over to him.

"Morgan, Morgan, I need to talk to you," she said, out of breath.

Sensing something was wrong, he pulled her to the side, out of sight of all the cameras flashing and news reporters.

"What's wrong, and what are you doing here?" he asked.

"The one who shot the governor is the one that raped me. I saw his face on the news," she told Morgan.

"What are you talking about? What guy on TV?" he replied.

126

Morgan didn't know what she was talking about because he never heard anything about who it was in police custody. All he knew was a man was shot by the local authorities and was now at Jefferson Hospital in critical condition.

"That man that shot your boss is the one who raped me. I will never forget his face. I loaded it to my phone from the website," she said, showing him the photo that was all over the news.

It wasn't until he saw the picture that he realized who she was talking about. His face was expressionless, as he didn't show emotion. "How the hell did he know my wife?" he thought to himself.

"You sure this is the guy?" he asked, staring at the man he hired to kill the person who was extorting him.

"I'm positive that's the guy. Let's go to the police so I can let them know," she stated, walking away toward the group of officers.

Morgan grabbed her arm and pulled her back.

"Wait, Carla, let me handle this. He's not gonna make it anyway. They said he'd be dead by tomorrow."

Carla was puzzled by his hesitation. She wanted to file a complaint, but he didn't want her to. She thought maybe he was going to handle everything and just for once in a long time was showing that he still loved her.

"So you will let them know what he did to me and make sure that he pays?" she asked skeptically.

"I'm going to take care of everything. Why don't you just go on home, and I'll see you when I finish up here."

Carla was a combination of scared and angry because she finally saw her attacker, and her husband was acting like it was nothing. She reluctantly left and headed back home thinking that everything would be all right. Something inside of her wanted to see the man who raped her, face-to-face.

Morgan stormed out of the hospital trying to take in what his wife just told him. He was wondering what made him target her and if that was how she contracted the virus. He needed some answers, so he drove over to the hospital that Kyle was at. Security was tight, and there were also reporters there trying to be the first to deliver the news of the suspect's condition. Being acting governor got Morgan past everyone.

"Leave us alone," he demanded, entering Kyle's room. The officer that was standing guard left. Morgan walked up to Kyle's bed and slapped the shit out of him. "I just want to know one thing: what did my wife have to do with anything?"

Kyle gave him a sinister smile as he licked the blood that was on his lip.

"She was a pawn in the game. You should have paid me my money, and nothing would have happened to her."

"Our business was over. She had nothing to do with it. I should kill you right now, and no one would ever know," he stated.

"See, that's where you're wrong. I have every conversation we had on tape. Anything happens, and you go down, so see, I'm still very much in charge. I just put you where you wanted to be. Now get me out of here so I can get far away, and you'll never have to worry about me again. I also want a half a million dollars for my vacation."

"I can't just get that kind of money without raising a red flag as to why. You gave my wife HIV, and now things will never be the same between us," Morgan said.

130

"I don't care about any of that. Just get me out of here 'cause if I see a jail cell, guess who will be joining me? Oh, and by the way, the person that was blackmailing you was your wife's piano instructor. I guess him and your wife had a thing. I can see why too. She has some good pussy, and it's so sweet," Kyle replied, laughing.

Morgan couldn't do a damn thing about it. He was in a big mess, and the man laughing at him had the upper hand. Without that evidence, he had to do exactly what he said. He even imagined Rapheal bending Carla over, plowing her from behind. He shook the image out of his head.

"I'll set something up to get you out of here tonight. Be ready. I don't care if you're still in pain or not," he stated.

"That's a good boy. Now get out of my room," Kyle said as he watched Morgan turn to leave. "Hey, Mr. Governor."

Morgan turned around to see what he wanted. "Give the misses my regards," he said, flicking his tongue in and out of his mouth.

If Morgan had had a gun, Kyle probably would be dead right now. He left, wondering how he was going to get him out. What he didn't know was the cops already had the tapes.

SALEENA AND HER FRIEND were sitting at a café not far from the hotel she was staying at, eating lunch. She was in heaven, watching the delectable chocolate delicacies being paraded in front of her on a electroplated silver platter. There were raspberry filled truffles and chocolate fondue with ripe, plump strawberries patiently waiting to be devoured. Saleena sank her pearly whites into the richness of the milk chocolate caressing a sweet strawberry as she listened to a couple at the next table arguing about their meal.

She was looking at her friend, who was wondering why she so urgently needed to meet up today.

"So what's on your mind?"

"I don't want to go through with this anymore," Saleena stated. "Things have gotten out of hand. I want out."

"What do you mean you want out? This was your idea to do this in the first place. I never wanted to be involved with this, and I sure didn't want to hurt anyone, but we did," her friend replied.

"No, *you* did!" Saleena corrected her, remembering that night when everything went wrong.

When she and Kevin went on their first date, she secretly stole his house key from him while they were having sex outside on the car. She waited for a few months before they decided to rob him for his valuables.

That night Saleena called Kevin asking to meet up with him, but he said that he would be gone until tomorrow. She took that as the perfect opportunity for them to rob his house. She called her friend, and she met her there. It looked like no one was home,

NAUGHTY HOUSEWIVES 2

so they went right in looking for any valuable they could find. As they were downstairs, Michelle heard a noise and thought it was Kevin coming home. She slipped her robe on and headed downstairs.

Saleena heard someone approaching and hid behind the door to the basement. He friend wasn't able to react fast enough, so she pulled out the pistol she was carrying. Thinking she was in trouble, she fired two rounds at the shadow on the stairs. Michelle fell down the rest of the steps. Saleena's friend then heard a second person and fired again, hitting whoever it was. Not trying to stick around, she grabbed Saleena, and they both fled the scene without taking anything. The guilt had been haunting Saleena ever since.

When Saleena hooked up with Kevin after that, she thought she would be able to still somehow manage to look him in the face, but it was hard. So when her friend called her while she was at dinner

135

and told her about something coming up, she used that to get out of there.

"We both had something to do with that, so we have to be careful and not implicate ourselves," Saleena's friend said, snapping Saleena out of the nightmare she was reliving.

"I don't want to see him anymore. Can't we just get out of here, before he finds out?" Saleena asked.

Saleena's friend slid over closer to her, placing her hands underneath the table between her thighs. She closed her eyes while she played with her pussy through the fabric of her panties. Saleena moaned when she stuck a finger inside and rotated it. Her pussy was so wet that it started making squirting sounds. She leaned toward her ear, bit it, then whispered: "Mommy, just hold off a little while longer, okay? I'll quit my job, and we can go wherever you like."

"Ooooh," Saleena moaned, enjoying the feeling taking over her body. The feeling and the sound of her friend's finger going in and out of Saleena's pussy made her cum within minutes. Saleena opened her eyes and noticed that a few wide-eyed Caucasians signaled disapproval with their condescending stares before returning their focus to whatever they were doing.

"Come on, let's get out of here. We have an audience," she stated, getting up. Saleena left with a smile on her face.

~ ~ ~ ~

"Remember when I told the both of you about the guy I hired to find out who was extorting me? Well it has resurfaced again, but now it's even worse," Morgan sighed as he, Marcus, and Kevin talked outside his house.

They couldn't risk talking inside, just in case the place was bugged. Kevin let Marcus crash at his place with him after he told him everything that went down at his house. Of course, leaving out the fact that he forced Akiylah to have sex with him numerous times.

"What is he asking for this time?" Kevin asked.

"It's not what he's asking for, but more or less what he's done. He has wrecked my marriage completely."

Morgan told them the whole story about everything that went down between him, Kyle, and his wife. They just listened with their mouths wide open. They were at a loss for words and realized that Morgan was in deeper than they thought.

"Do you have any idea where this guy lives or where he would keep the tapes?"

"No," Morgan said, shaking his head. "It's impossible for me to get him out of there. He shot the governor, and that's the fed's case. If I had those tapes, he could burn in hell for all I care. Shit, I would light the match."

"You need a lawyer 'cause you're in a pretty bad predicament right now, and you need to start thinking legal strategies," Marcus replied.

"We will help you as much as we can, but remember, we are ball players, man. The whole world is watching us also," Kevin complained.

Just when they thought it couldn't get any worse, an unmarked car pulled up, followed by a patrol car. Det. Davis stepped out of the driver's seat and walked up to Morgan.

"Excuse me, Mr. Governor. I need you to come with me. It's important, and I'll have you back in an hour."

"Do I need a lawyer?" Morgan questioned.

"Only if you think you need one." The detective smirked.

"Fine, let's go," he stated. He looked at Kevin and Marcus, then nodded his head, letting them know to have his lawyer meet them at the station. He got into the car, and they drove away.

~ ~ ~ ~

They arrived at the station about twenty minutes later. Det. Davis escorted Morgan to one of the interview rooms and then went to see if his partner had come back yet.

"Has anyone seen Hill yet?" he asked everyone sitting at their desk. They all shook their heads and continued working.

He called her cell phone but got no answer. He decided to just to take care of it himself. He figured she was still tied up with helping her mom.

"I don't want to take up too much of your time, Governor, so I will get straight to the point," Davis said, trying to read Morgan's expression. When he couldn't, he continued. "I talked to a Raquel Jackson, and she gave me some interesting news."

"I don't know no Raquel Jac—"

"Before you finish that statement, she also supplied us with this," he told him, pressing play on the DVD player.

Morgan watched the video of him and Symira having sex, then looked at Det. Davis.

"So what? A man and woman can't have consensual sex? What, is that a crime, Detective?"

"It is if someone says this," he stated, playing the recorder.

When Morgan heard that, his heart skipped a beat. He was wondering exactly how much the detective knew. There was enough evidence on that tape to send him away for a long time. He needed to figure a way out of this one. As soon as Det. Davis stopped the recorder, Morgan tried to explain.

"I was being extorted, and I needed someone to find out who was doing it. I didn't tell him to kill anybody. What I meant by ice was 'put in prison.'"

"Would you like a lawyer? 'Cause I don't want you to incriminate yourself," he asked Morgan.

"I have nothing to hide. I'll give you a statement if it will clear all of this up," Morgan replied.

Soon as Morgan was about to start talking, his lawyer walked in ceasing all communication. Kevin had called the best lawyer Pennsylvania had to offer, and he wasted no time taking action.

"Anything my client has said up to this point should be erased. You should not have been questioning him without legal representation," Lou Savino stated. "If you're not charging him with anything, we will be leaving."

"I didn't force him to talk to me. He came in of his own free will. Can I charge him with something as of now, yes, but will I, no. You see he is still the acting governor, so I have to be one hundred percent sure if I go that route. By law, I'm supposed to hand what I know over to the feds, but I won't," he stated.

Detective Davis took the cassette out of the recorder, then broke it in half. He passed it to Morgan, then opened the door, motioning for them to leave. Before they left, he said: "Governor, I will need to speak with you at a later date. I'll call your office to set up an appointment."

Morgan nodded, then followed his lawyer out of the building and to his car. He drove Morgan back to his house.

"I don't know what just happened back there, but you may not yet be in the clear. He wants something, but what?" Savino stated.

"I will definitely let you know when I find out. Thank you for the ride," he said, before exiting the car.

Morgan knew exactly what the detective may want. Because of what he had done, Morgan was willing to comply.

~ ~ ~ ~

"How long will y'all be gone for?" Sasha asked her son, dropping him and Akiylah off at the airport.

"Only a week or two, Mom. She just wants to see her family and friends 'cause she misses them. I will call you once we get there to let you know we're safe," Sahmeer said as they check their luggage in with the baggage handlers.

"Make sure you do that. I love y'all," she replied, giving both of them hugs.

"We love you too," they both said in unison.

Sahmeer hadn't talked to his father since that day he caught him trying to hit on Akiylah. Even though she tried to say he was drunk, it still meant nothing to him. She didn't like seeing their family torn apart because of her. That's why she wanted to go back to the Virgin Islands to see her own family. She promised herself that she would tell him the truth once they got settled there. They boarded the plane and took their seats in first class.

"Are you okay?" he asked, leaning over and giving her a romantic kiss on the lips.

She kissed him back and nodded her head yes. She looked out the window as the plane took off down the runway. Once the plane was in the air, the fasten seatbelt light went out, and everyone was able to move around freely.

"Would you like something to drink?" a gorgeous stewardess asked them. Sahmeer couldn't stop looking at how perky her titties were.

She was so beautiful, with a supermodel body. He ordered a couple of drinks, and she rushed off to get them. Sahmeer was hard just from watching her switch away. He reached over and tried to stick his hand inside Akiylah's tights. She stopped him by slapping his hand.

"Me friend is here," she said, smiling at him. "She goes away in two days, okay?"

He leaned back in his chair. He needed to get one off right now. That feeling just wouldn't go away.

"I have to use the bathroom. Are you okay?" he asked her.

"Yes, me gonna take a nap for awhile," she replied.

Sahmeer got up and walked toward the back in search of the bathroom. He walked past the sexy stewardess and smiled at her.

"Is there anything I can help you with?" she asked. For some reason, Sahmeer thought she was flirting with him, and wanted to be sure.

"It all depends on what you're offering," he stated, getting a little close.

"This is clearly unorthodox and inappropriate, sir. Can you please back up?"she said, offended.

"I was just playing with you," Sahmeer said apologetically, and walked to the bathroom.

He sat down on the toilet and loosened his shorts. Next he pulled out his penis and started massaging it, bringing it to attention. He closed his eyes, imagining that it was the pretty lady's mouth wrapped around it. He started pumping faster, as he felt himself ready to explode. Just as he was getting to the point of no return, there was a tap on the door.

"Sahmeer, open the door."

He unlocked the door, and Akiylah walked in with a smile on her face. She just stared at him holding his dick in his hand.

"Need some help?" she chuckled devilishly.

"Um, well he needs a kiss." He grinned mischievously while holding his penis.

"Oh, me can do that," she said, her eyes revealing the naughty thoughts filling her head while she scooted down and took his full length into her watery mouth.

Feverishly, she sucked and pumped him with her hands simultaneously until the load that coated her tonsils glided down her throat. She drank every bit of it, then licked her lips. "That was some good protein me just had," she told him, rinsing her mouth out.

They went back to their seats and relaxed until they reached their destination. The stewardess never even mentioned anything about what Sahmeer had tried to do. She kept her professionalism, and he gave her a hefty tip when they exited the plane. Sahmeer waited patiently for their suitcases to show up on the luggage conveyor. Then they took the taxi to the awaiting yacht that would take them to the island.

When they reached the island, Sahmeer couldn't take his eyes off of how beautiful it was. The water was crystal clear, and there were so many beautiful women that he thought he had died and had gone to heaven. Akiylah spotted her mom and sister, and they rushed into each other's arms. Her sister was the spitting image of her. Sahmeer thought he was looking at twins. Their mom also looked like she was only twenty-five. He could tell that she was even more beautiful when she was younger. After Akiylah introduced them to Sahmeer, they all hugged and headed home.

Akiylah's mother had prepared an extravagant meal for their guest. The smell hit his nose as soon as she opened the door. The table was full of different Caribbean dishes.

"Sit down. Me make you a plate," Matea called out to Sahmeer.

Akiylah and her sister took their suitcases up to the room, then returned to join them. They ate and talked for what seemed like an hour. Sahmeer enjoyed his wife's family. Everyone seemed happy to be around one another. He missed having that relationship with his own family. Against his better judgment, he decided that when he returned home, he would try to reconcile with his dad. Nothing had ever come between them, and he hoped that it didn't happen again.

"Thank you so much for the food. I'm stuffed and exhausted now," Sahmeer said.

"You welcome, me dear. You can go to your room and rest now if you like," Matea replied.

Akiylah showed him which room they would be staying in, then returned to the kitchen to help clean up and catch up on everything. She enjoyed being back home. Tomorrow she was going to show Sahmeer the beach she grew up on.

Ten

SYMIRA AND HER HUSBAND had just finished having wild sex not once but twice. She felt like she had to make up for lost time. Actually, it was Morgan who suggested it because they had been spending too much time together. She hadn't been intimate with her husband in almost two months. Every time he would try, she would make up some excuse about her period coming on because of birth control or that she had a bladder infection. The truth was she'd been having too much sex but with another man. Morgan thought that by Symira having some fun with her husband, it would throw him off their affair, and he wouldn't get suspicious.

They both took a shower together and were now in their bedroom watching the season finale of

Empire. Since they had missed it the night before, they decided to catch it on Netflix.

"I have to watch this season from the beginning 'cause Twitter and Instagram have been blowing up about it," Symira said as she lay in his arms.

"It's pretty good," he replied. "I'm just glad that you're actually home tonight and not at work late."

"Well my boss gave me the night and tomorrow off, so we can do something together. I know he's probably missing my work right now, but he'll manage," she said, thinking about them fucking in some hotel. When she and her husband were having sex, she thought it was Morgan. That's why she was able to go more than one round.

"How does it feel being the governor's secretary now?"

"It has its perks," she smiled.

Her cell phone rang just as the show was going off. She saw that it was Morgan's number.

"I'll be right back. That's him calling now. Probably can't find something," she said, trying to rush out of the room. She ran downstairs, answering it on the way. "Hey, baby, you missing this pussy already? We only fucked twice, but I thought about you the whole time."

"Awww, how sweet. I was thinking about you too. In fact, that's the reason I'm calling you now."

Symira looked at the phone, making sure she was talking to the right person, with a look of confusion on her face.

"Hello?" she said softly.

"See, that's what you should have said the first time, before you started talking too much," Carla sneered.

Symira was silent because she didn't know what to say. She wanted to smack herself because she knew Carla was right.

"Look, I didn't call you to talk about you and Morgan. I just called to let your husband know that I still have his shirt from the other night. I'll drop it by the office tomorrow so you can give it to him."

"What the hell are you talking about?" Symira asked, confused.

"I'll tell you what I'm talking about. He ripped my shirt off of me the other night while we were making love in your bed. It felt good to have a man touching me again since I found out that I was HIV-positive. I assume you know that already from my husband, and since he hasn't touched me since, I thought your husband needed to be touched also. So while you were fucking my husband, I was fucking yours," Carla blurted out without any remorse.

Symira thought about what she said, and tears began falling from her eyes. It wasn't the fact that Carla had sex with her husband; it was because she knew Carla was HIV-positive and she may have just exposed herself to it when she fucked her husband.

"Please say you wouldn't do that to me?" Symira begged, hoping it was a joke.

"Payback is a bitch. How do you like that?" Carla hung up the phone before Symira even had a chance to respond.

"No, no, no," she screamed, throwing her phone against the wall.

Greg heard the noise and walked down the steps. He walked up to Symira and touched her shoulder.

"What's wrong?" he asked.

"Get off of me! Don't you even touch me."

"What are you talking about?"

Symira moved away from him. "I can't believe this. How could you fuck her and risk the chance of getting infected?"

"Infected? What the hell are you talking about? Who did I fuck?" Greg asked, not knowing what she was talking about.

"That bitch said she still has your shirt and the other night was great. Then you gonna have sex with me? Are you out of your mind? I can't believe this is happening to me. Oh my God. Please don't let me be infected, please," she sobbed even louder.

"Who are you talking about?" Greg said, trying to remember who he had sex with.

"Carla, my boss's wife."

He suddenly remembered the strange female that was in his bed. The one he thought was Symira.

"Yeah, I see you remember now. Did you at least wear a condom when you fucked her?"

He thought about that night and realized that he didn't use any protection. He even remembered the time when they went to her house and Symira was having sex with her while he watched, then joined in. He also remembered when his wife told him that her boss's wife was raped and the rapist gave her the virus.

"What are you thinking about, Greg? Then you even had the nerve to fuck her in our bed?"

"I thought it was you, baby. I'm sorry," he pleaded.

"Well since you want to be sticking your thing in everybody, I need to tell you something. I've also been fucking around on you. As a matter of fact, I've been sleeping with my boss."

Greg smacked the shit out of her. Symira fell on the couch. He went upstairs, grabbed some clothes, and left. Symira called Morgan to tell him what just happened, but it said her number was blocked. She sat on the couch and cried until she fell asleep.

~ ~ ~ ~

Morgan was sitting in his office signing some papers that were left on his desk, when Symira

157

walked in. After she shut the door and turned toward Morgan, he could see that she had been crying for a while. He stood up and started toward her, thinking that her husband had done something to her.

"What's wrong, baby?" he asked, putting his arms around her. He pulled her to his chest, and she started sobbing uncontrollably again. "Talk to me. What did he do this time?"

She pushed away from him and just looked into his eyes, searching for anything that said he knew what happened, but couldn't find anything.

"Your wife may have just ruined our lives, and I don't know what to do," she pouted.

"What happened?"

"She slept with my husband a couple of days ago, then called me rubbing it in."

"What?" he said, running his fingers through his hair. "Leave him, then, and we can be together

158

without worrying about them anymore. Ain't that what we talked about, us leaving them for each other?"

"It's not that simple, Morgan. We can't be together until I find out what's going on."

"What are you talking about? I haven't been happy with my wife for a while now. We haven't even been sleeping in the same bed. Our marriage is practically over."

"I'm talking about with me. I slept with my husband, remember? There's a chance that he may have it and passed it on to me. If that's the case, there is no more us. Don't you understand?" she said, sitting down on the couch.

Morgan forgot that he had suggested that she sleep with him. He didn't think she would do it, though. Now he knew he couldn't risk having sex with her until they got the results from her test back.

"When are you going to get tested?" he asked.

159

"I went this morning before I came here. It was negative for now, but I have to wait for six months to know for sure. The doctor said it could take a year for the symptoms to show, before I can be cleared."

Morgan loved Symira, but he wasn't trying to die. As much as he knew it would hurt her, he had to cut his ties with her. He had so many questions bottled up inside, but he refrained from verbalizing any of them at this time.

"We can't be together anymore, Symira, 'cause I don't want to risk getting infected. That's why I'm not with my wife anymore," he said.

"So you're just . . ."

"Wait, let me finish," he said, putting up his hand. "If everything works out and you're not infected, then we can start a life together. Just let me know when you find out."

160

Symira looked for some kind of smile or anything saying that he was joking, but found nothing. She didn't say a word, just got up and walked out of his office. It took every part of his manly nature not to break down crying at that moment. He had lost his wife and the girl he fell in love with. He blamed everything on Carla instead of putting the blame on himself. Morgan grabbed his suit jacket and stormed out the door. Everything seemed to be falling apart right before his eyes.

"Governor," someone yelled out to him as he was getting into his car. He turned around to see Det. Davis approaching.

"Damn it, not today," he thought to himself. "What can I do for you, Detective? I'm kind of in a hurry."

"I just needed to run something by you real quick. I understand that you will be leaving for Harrisburg full time now, and I need you to put in a word with my boss for me," Det. Davis said, puffing on a cigarette.

"Send me an email, and I will take care of it. Now I have to get out of here," Morgan stated, getting into his car and pulling out.

When Morgan arrived home, Carla was in the kitchen washing dishes. He stared at her for a minute before he even said anything.

"How could you do that? Are you that heartless?" he said, getting her attention.

Carla just kept doing the dishes like she didn't even hear him talking.

"Did you hear what the hell I just said?" he shouted, spinning her around.

"Keep your hands off of me. It's funny how you're worried more about your little whore than your own wife. You haven't slept in the same bed as me or even asked me how I'm feeling. You weren't even worried about me when I was raped, drugged, and given this disease that I can't get rid of, so fuck you and that little bitch. Yes, I'm that heartless, and I hope you fucked her too. It would serve your ass good also," Carla snapped.

As she talked, tears formed in her eyes. Morgan knew at that point that the love he once had for her was gone, because he didn't care about those tears.

"I'm leaving for Harrisburg in the morning. I will be staying there, so you can keep this house. I'm sorry that it has to be this way." He chortled on his way upstairs.

"Don't worry, the newspapers will have a field day with your little affair." She laughed.

Morgan walked back downstairs. He knew if that got out, he would surely suffer if he wanted to stay governor.

"I'm begging you, please don't do this. I'll give you anything you want. I won't fight it if you ask for half of everything. Just don't make this any messier than it already is."

"You already made your bed. Now lie in it. Talk to my lawyers 'cause I'm done talking. Goodbye," she said, then walked away from him, leaving him speechless.

~ ~ ~ ~

Sasha had been spending the last few nights alone. With everybody gone, it gave her a lot of "me time." She was sitting in the hot tub listening to the soothing sound of Joe as his voice helped her escape to another place: "Let's make a love scene, steamy and true, erotic memories for an audience of two. And we'll make a love scene, let the foreplay begin, and replay each moment again, and again, and again."

Her hand started making its way between her legs as she closed her eyes and played with her clit. She enjoyed playing with herself. No one could make her cum the way she could make herself cum. Between the thrusters from the hot tub and her fingers, Sasha had one of the biggest orgasms ever. She smiled as her hand continued to massage her clit, causing friction in her vagina. Sasha was sexually frustrated and needed this so bad. After a couple more orgasms, she opened her eyes and smiled. She got out of the hot tub and went into the bedroom and fell asleep.

~ ~ ~ ~

Around three o'clock in the morning, Sasha received a call that Sahmeer had gotten into an accident in the Virgin Islands. Sasha immediately called Marcus to inform him of what had happened. When she told him, he jumped up and ran over to the house. They sat patiently waiting to hear something from Akiylah.

"Please let my baby be alright," Sasha sniffled. She was rocking back and forth in her seat. Marcus sat next to her and put his arm around her.

"Our son is as strong as they come. It was only a shark bite. I'm quite sure it's not that bad. If it was, she would have told us. Calm down, ma; I got you."

Sasha was hoping that he was right, but something kept eating away at her. Call it mother's intuition, but she had a feeling that it was much worse.

"Would you like some coffee?" she asked, getting up and walking toward the kitchen.

"That would be nice, thank you," he replied, stretching.

She poured them both a cup, then came back and sat down next to him. Sasha watched Marcus sip his coffee and realized how much she missed him.

"Did you really do that to Akiylah?" she asked. She just wanted to hear the truth, not a lie.

He looked at her, then held his head down. She knew his hesitation to explicate could only be attributed to his guilt, the kind of guilt that can cause one to implode. She had the answer before he could say anything.

"Yes, that happened, but I was intoxicated," he said, trying to still use that excuse.

Sasha could see that he was sorry, and she also was because of her own affairs. She wanted to tell him but chose not to say anything. She leaned over and gave him a kiss on the cheek.

"I forgive you, Marcus. It's up to our son to do the same. We can get past this," she said.

"I sure hope so, because I miss our family," he replied, looking at the see-through nightgown she was wearing. Her titties looked perky as hell, trying to escape the fabric that was hiding them.

Sasha noticed what he was looking at and laughed. She hit him in the arm playfully.

"I guess you do miss me, huh?"

"No," he said, getting up and sitting on the other couch. He picked up the magazine on the table and acted like he was reading it. He didn't want Sasha to see the hunger for her in his eyes.

"What's wrong, you don't want this pussy anymore?" She rubbed her fingers between her thighs. She lifted her legs in the air to give him a better view of her plump vagina lips. Marcus was so flabbergasted that he couldn't respond. She got up and walked over to where he was sitting. Sasha bent down and began unbuckling his belt, squeezing his limpness through the crotch of his jeans.

"I want you to fuck me right now and take our pain away for the moment," she said with pleading eyes.

Marcus couldn't resist her touch. He lifted her up onto his lap. Sasha lifted her nightgown over her head. At the same time, Marcus was releasing his erection from confinement. He gently eased inside of her, taking her breath away.

"I miss you so much," she moaned, trying to reach her climax.

Just as they were getting into it, the phone rang. Thinking that something else was wrong, Sasha rushed to answer it, leaving Marcus holding a hard dick in his hand.

"Hello," Sasha said, pressing the talk button.

"Hi, this is University Hospital. Your son will be arriving here by helicopter within the next thirty minutes. If you would like to be here when he comes, you can leave now, and I'll be waiting for you," the nurse said.

"We're on our way."

Sasha hung up the phone and rushed upstairs to throw some clothes on. Marcus fixed his clothes and waited for Sasha to return. When she came back down, they headed out the door.

When they entered the hospital, patients were waiting their turn in the triage room, and doctors in green scrubs or white lab coats were leisurely standing around the emergency room area.

They walked up to the desk, hoping to get information. After a couple of minutes, one of the doctors came over to talk to them.

"Hi, I'm Doctor Katz. Would you follow me so we can talk?" he said. They followed him to his office, and once everyone was inside and seated, he began. "He was bitten by a great white shark after falling from a barge of some sort. He's gonna need a blood transfusion because he lost a lot of blood. He also sustained severe head trauma, and he's going to be transferred to the ICU as soon as he arrives. He'll need to be observed before we'll know anything definite, although there are hematomas present."

"What's that?" Sasha asked.

"That means there's bleeding in the brain, but don't worry, he is responsive from what the medics were telling me, and isn't in a coma yet," the doctor replied.

"Oh God. Can we be tested to see if we are a match?" Marcus asked the doctor.

"Yes, we can get started on that right away. I was going to suggest that next. If you will follow me, sir, and I will have one of the nurses handle you, ma'am."

Sasha was about to say something, but Marcus and the doctor rushed off before she had a chance to. Sasha got really nervous and started shaking in her seat. The nurse came and escorted her to the lab to get started.

Eleven

"WE HAVE TO HURRY up and get all the money and valuables now. He won't be back home for a while. I talked to him earlier," Saleena said as they pulled into the gated area. They were able to get through with no problem because the security knew her friend.

"Okay, let's do it and hurry up out of here. I have some last-minute arrangements to take care of. Then we can be out of here together tonight," Cynthia said, rubbing on Saleena's leg. It made Saleena wet instantly.

They parked and exited the car. They went through the back door because they knew it would be open. As they entered the house, Saleena headed for the bedroom. She walked in and opened the drawers. There was so much jewelry inside that her eyes lit up. She put it all in a pillow case, then opened up the closet. When she moved the clothes out of the way, the little safe was on the floor.

"I found the safe. Get up here," Saleena shouted.

Cynthia came up the steps quickly and met Saleena in the room.

"Help me lift it up and get it into the car. I know there's enough money in here that we will be set for a long time."

As soon as they lifted the safe, it set off a motion sensor which triggered a silent alarm. They didn't even know it happened.

"I knew we could do it," Cynthia said as they put the safe in the car. "Let's get whatever else we can find. I have someone who is going to pay big for the trophies and jewelry."

They searched for everything they could find that was worth something, which in this house was almost everything. They wished they had brought a truck, but they knew that would be too suspicious.

~ ~ ~ ~

Detective Davis was on his way to work after a well-deserved sleep. He had been working double time trying to solve his open cases. One was already closed, and another one was coming along. He stopped at Dunkin Donuts on City Line Avenue to grab a coffee and a couple of donuts.

When he got back in his car, dispatch was trying to get in touch with him.

"Dispatch to Detective Davis, come in."

"This is Detective Davis, go ahead," he said, taking a bite of his donut.

"Please call the desk ASAP."

He pulled out his cell phone and called the front desk. Usually that meant a CI needed to speak to him.

"Hello, 39th Precinct. This is Sergeant Dunbar," the desk sergeant said politely.

"Detective, we just received a silent alarm call over the radio a few minutes ago. Security went to check it out and said that police were already on the scene. We thought you were there."

"Why would I be there?"

"The guy said one of the officers was the one that was searching for one of the resident's wife's killer. He said it was a female cop."

Det. Davis was wondering what his partner would be doing there at this time. He tried calling her cell phone, but it went straight to voicemail.

"I'm close to the area. I'll go past there and see what's going on," he told dispatch over the radio.

"Ten-four, sir."

Detective Davis thought Detective Hill had found a lead and had gone to check it out. He hadn't talked to her all day, so he assumed it was a spur of the moment thing. On his way there, another call came over the radio that two suspicious people were carrying a bunch of things out of a house and it looked like they were robbing the place. He radioed in for the address, and it was the same one his partner was at. That was strange to him, so thinking his partner was in trouble, he hit the sirens and stepped on the gas.

He arrived just as the security guard was getting out of his truck. Detective Davis exited his car and motioned for the security guard to stay down.

"Did you see anyone come out yet?" he asked, putting on his police logo jacket.

"No, sir. No one came out yet."

"Okay, I want you to stay here, and whatever happens, stay out of my way. They may be holding my partner hostage, and I don't need some rent-a-cop in harm's way."

The security guard looked at the detective with a look of disgust, but stayed put. Detective Davis pulled his weapon from his shoulder holster and headed toward the open door. Just as he was about to enter, someone was exiting.

"Freeze, police!" he shouted, aiming his gun at the suspect.

The suspect dropped the suitcase and raised her hands in the air. They both stared at each other momentarily, not sure what to say or do. Detective Davis was shocked at the person standing before his own two eyes. Knowing he had a job to do, he snapped out of his moment of shock.

"Turn around and put your hands behind your head," he stated firmly.

"So you're gonna arrest me before you even ask what I'm doing here?" she said, looking at him.

"Just turn around and place your hands behind your head. I will not say it again," he said for the second time.

"I have to show you something," she said, reaching into her right pocket.

"Don't move," he shouted.

Before she could lift her hand out, Detective Davis shot her. She fell back into the house. He ran up on her with his gun still aimed, but she was already dead. He bent down to see what she was reaching for in her pocket, when he heard someone else approaching at a fast pace. He took cover behind the wall of the door frame. He took a deep breath, then jumped behind the wall with his gun aimed.

"Don't move, police!"

They both had their guns locked on each other, waiting for someone to make a move. There was a lot of tension in the air for what seemed like forever.

"What the hell is going on here?" Detective Davis asked, looking at the second suspect.

She didn't say anything. Instead she dropped her gun and looked at the body lying still on the floor. Tears came flowing down as she knelt down and lifted the woman's head into her chest.

"I'm sorry. I'm so sorry," she said, kissing her on the forehead.

As Detective Davis stood there, so many questions raced through his mind. He watched as his partner incoherently sat motionless next to the body on the floor. He lowered his gun, thinking that the threat was over.

"Who is this woman, Cynthia?" he asked. "And what is going on here?"

She looked at her partner, and before she could say anything, there were two shots out of nowhere.

179

Detective Davis felt his chest and looked at his hand. It was covered in blood as he dropped to his knees, then fell to the floor. Detective Hill looked up and saw the security guard standing in the doorway with a smoking gun in his hand.

Franco had been working as a security guard for a year and a half for the gated community. He and Saleena had been robbing houses the whole time, but they never took a lot. About a year ago, Saleena met Cynthia at a café, and the two instantly hit it off. They explored each other's bodies, and Saleena turned her out.

One day Cynthia was responding to a robbery call, and when she got there, Saleena was walking out with the bag of money. Cynthia watched speechless as Saleena hopped into the awaiting car and fled the crime scene. Reluctantly she let them get away. Later that night, while they affectionately lay in bed, she brought up the robbery. She informed Saleena that she wanted in and that she would keep the heat off of them as long as she could. Saleena told her that she would have to talk to her boyfriend about it and that she would let her know.

Cynthia didn't like the fact that she had a boyfriend, but she went along with it. She wanted Saleena all to herself. She had fallen in love with her that fast. They made love for a few hours, then Saleena left. The next day she called Cynthia and told her she had a deal and she would see her when she returned from out of town.

Saleena was in Washington, DC, handling some business. When she was getting off the elevator, she recognized the man getting on but didn't say anything. It wasn't until a week or two later, when she saw him again at the post office, that they spoke to each other. They had a date and had sex on the hood of the car. She told Cynthia all about it one night, and it made her come up with the idea to rob him. The night they went to do it, everything went wrong, and someone ended up getting killed. Cynthia felt bad and went over to his house to see how he was doing. She pretended like she had some more questions for him, but when she saw the bulge in his pants, she wanted something else. Thinking back to what Saleena had told her, she ended up having sex with him until he called out his wife's name. That really made her feel guilty, so she left.

Franco spotted the right opportunity, and he called Saleena to set up the heist again. This time, they had almost gotten away with everything, if it hadn't been for that silent alarm. He still thought it was taken care of by telling the police there was a cop on the scene already. Then Detective Davis showed up and not only ruined everything but killed Franco's girlfriend in the process.

"Come on, the cops are coming. We have to get out of here now," Franco stated, as he saw Cynthia still crying. He thought they had been having an affair, but the look on her face confirmed it.

Cynthia glanced up at him momentarily, then looked at her partner lying in a pool of blood. She really loved her partner like a brother, and now he was lying there dying from trying to save her. She felt like it was all Franco's fault that they were in this predicament. If he wouldn't have let her partner get to the house, Saleena and Pete would still be alive. She looked around for her gun, and when she spotted it, she went to reach for it. Franco turned to look out the door when he heard a bunch of sirens approaching.

"Come the hell on. The cops are—" he said, turning around and staring at the gun aimed at him. "What are you doing?"

"Police, drop the gun," she shouted, hoping someone heard her outside.

Knowing what was about to happen, he tried to get off a shot first. It was wide, and Detective Hill hit him three times in the chest. He fell out the door, dying instantly. She stood up and headed for the door, when someone grabbed her leg. She looked down and saw that Detective Davis was still alive.

"Pete?" she asked, kneeling down toward her partner. The sirens stopped, and she heard footsteps approaching. "We have an officer down. Get a bus here now!"

By the time the ambulance arrived, Det. Davis was still showing signs of consciousness. They put him in the back, with Det. Hill right behind them, and sped off to the emergency room. Det. Davis watched his partner staring at him with tears in her eyes. He reached out for her hand. She grabbed his and squeezed it tightly into hers. He pulled her closer to him so the medic couldn't hear him.

"Whatever happens, I got your back," he whispered in her ear before passing out.

Epilogue

SASHA AND MARCUS SAT in the room with their son all night hoping he would wake up. He had been fully sedated by the IV and medicine that was given to him. He had over a hundred stitches in his leg. He still wasn't in a coma, even though the doctor suggested that he be put in a medically induced one. Sasha refused because she needed to talk to her baby.

"Me brought you some coffee," Akiylah said, walking into the room with three cups in her hand.

"Hey," Sasha replied, standing up and giving her hug. Akiylah had just gotten there from the airport. "Why didn't you call me when you landed? I would have come and got you from the airport."

"Me didn't want to bother you," she said, leaning over and giving Sahmeer a kiss. She looked up and noticed that Marcus was staring at her. It wasn't in a lustful way, though. She walked over and gave him a hug. "He will be okay. Me pray for him."

That made Marcus break down for the first time. Sasha came over, and the three of them shared a painful moment. The doctor walked in as they were drying their eyes. The look on his face made them all look up.

"What is it, Doc?" Marcus asked, staring at him.

"Well, I don't know how to say this, sir," he sighed, holding his head down.

"Just say it."

"It seems that neither of you are a match for your son's blood type."

"What? That can't be right," Marcus said, with worry in his eyes. He walked over to the window holding his head. He turned around and looked at the doctor. "Are you sure?"

"Well, to make sure everything was drawn correctly, I'm going to have the phlebotomist draw a few more tubes of blood to be tested. She is on her way now."

"Okay," Marcus responded in confusion. "So how long will it take for the results to come back this time?"

Just then the nurse walked in with her equipment to take his blood. He sat down and let her do her job. He looked at the doctor to answer the question that he already asked a minute ago. Noticing the look on Marcus's face, the doctor answered him.

"I'm sending our blood back up stat, so it shouldn't take as long, because the first ones were tainted. In order to give the blood to your son, we have to ensure that everything is on point, or it could prove fatal for him," he said, taking notes on a chart in his hand before continuing.

"The ABO blood group typing test, which is a paternity/DNA test to determine your blood type and to ensure you are a match for your son, was compromised, and that's an important factor to ensure that your blood type matches for the transfusion process. Blood type A can only go to other As, and Bs can only go to Bs. If it's blood type O, you are a universal donor and can donate to anyone, but if the blood type is not compatible, very dangerous results will occur. So that's why we have to be careful."

Sasha's face looked like she had seen a ghost as she listened to the doctor talking. She wanted to say something but couldn't form the words. The doctor and nurse left to take care of everything, and Sasha, Marcus, and Akiylah patiently wait for them to come back. The doctor said it shouldn't take more than an hour or so. Anxiety was on everyone's face, and Sahmeer's life was at stake.

An hour later the doctor returned with a clipboard in his hand. They couldn't read his facial expression, so they just waited for the news. Sasha was the more nervous one out of the three.

"Hello, everyone, once again," the doctor spoke, with a gentle smile that had everyone on the edge of their seats. "I just wanted to talk to you about your blood test and your son."

"Okay. Is everything alright now? There weren't any complications this time, right?" Marcus asked, panicking a little.

"No, no, sir, there wasn't," he responded, trying to prepare his words correctly. "Well, after testing your blood once again, sir, and getting the same results, I knew we had a serious problem."

Marcus had a bad feeling about what the doctor was about to say, and so did Sasha. She knew exactly what was going on. Tears formed in her eyes, and before the doctor could say anything, she hit him with the news.

"Sahmeer is not your son," she blurted out.

Marcus turned around and looked at his wife. Akiylah looked up with shock on her face also. No one was ready for that kind of information. She had just dropped a bomb on everyone.

"What do you mean he's not my son?"

"I wanted to tell you a long time ago but just didn't know how. I'm sorry, Marcus. I never meant to hurt you like this," Sasha said as tears freely fell from her face.

Marcus felt like he was hyperventilating as he tried to process all of it. His mind started racing as he thought about all the years he had been misled. He just couldn't figure it out. Sahmeer looked just like him, the only difference being that he was light skinned, but Marcus blamed those features on Sasha.

"So who is the father, then?" he asked, not really wanting to know the answer.

"You are still his father, Marcus, and he needs you more than ever right now. Can we please just try to save our son?" she begged, walking over toward him. She tried to touch Marcus, but he pushed her hand away.

"I said, who is his father, Sasha?"

Just as she was about to say the name of Sahmeer's father, Kevin and Mike walked into the room. They both looked concerned and scared. Kevin walked over and gave Marcus a brotherly hug.

"How is he doing?" he asked after releasing his grasp.

"Not good at all," Marcus sighed. "It seems that I'm not a match to give him a blood transfusion, and neither is Sasha."

"What are you talking about? How can that be?"

"I'm not his father," he said as tears formed in his eyes for the second time today.

"So who is his father then?" Kevin asked, looking at Sasha for answers.

"You are," she told him, causing the whole room to become quiet. Everyone's mouth was wide open, including the doctor's.

"Dad, what is she talking about?" Mike said, walking over toward him. Now everyone was staring at Kevin for answers. He didn't have any, because he had a dumbfounded look on his face.

"Sasha, what are you talking about?"

"You know what I'm talking about," she yelled, getting louder than usual. "I only slept with two people in that time frame. That was you and Marcus."

Kevin turned to look at his friend. Marcus just stared at him, waiting to see what he had to say.

"That night I stayed over Michelle's, I woke up in the middle of the night." He started thinking back.

(March 1997)

Kevin got out of bed to grab something to drink from the kitchen. When he walked downstairs, Sasha was asleep on the couch. He walked past her, and he noticed that the blanket had fallen off of her and onto the floor. He walked over to pick it up, and when he looked down at her, she wasn't wearing anything but panties and a shirt. He tried not to stare, but his little head was thinking for his big head.

Sasha woke up still tipsy from the party she had come from, and saw Kevin watching her. Instead of covering up, she smiled at him, sticking her hand inside her panties. She began fingering her pussy, getting wetter by the second.

All Kevin could do was watch as she performed for him. His dick was at full erection from his hand finding its way down there. He stroked the outside of his boxer shorts, the whole time never taking his eyes off of Sasha.

She sat up on the couch and opened her legs to give him a better view of the show. Kevin looked at the stairs to make sure Michelle was still in her room, then got down on his knees in front of Sasha. He pulled her panties to the side and told her to lie back down on the couch. She put one leg on the back of the couch and the other on the floor as Kevin got comfortable between her legs.

He inserted two fingers into her and sucked on her clit softly, knowing that she liked it. She ground her pussy into his face, and her body shook as she released her juices into his mouth. Sasha started moaning like crazy, so he tried to cover her mouth to keep the noise down.

He pushed her legs up so they were touching her chest, and dipped his tongue into her asshole. She instantly exploded again from the excitement. After pleasing her, he needed to feel her insides. He pulled her body toward the edge of the couch and inserted his dick into her love tunnel. Sasha was in the zone now. She started rotating her hips to his every stroke. It felt so good that Kevin couldn't contain himself from erupting and shot his load all inside her.

When he pulled out, Sasha got down and sucked up all her juices from off of his dick. She even stuck her finger into her pussy and pulled out his semen, licking every bit off of each finger.

"Damn, that was good," he said, fixing his boxers. "I have to go back upstairs before Michelle wakes up."

"This stays between us, right?" Sasha asked, trying to wipe the couch off with her panties.

"Yes, and they can never find out about this."

Kevin rushed back upstairs and eased back into bed with Michelle. He didn't even go into the bathroom to wash off. As he lay there, though, he thought about how he didn't use protection with Sasha. He hoped that she didn't end up pregnant or, even worse, that neither of them caught anything.

"I didn't think we would end up marrying them or anything, Marcus. I'm sorry, bro," he said, coming back to the here and now.

Marcus took in what Kevin just told him. He wasn't mad at his friend; he was more concerned about the fact that Sahmeer wasn't his. All that played through his head, and it truly hurt him. Right now, though, it was more about saving his son's life.

"Look, I'm not mad at you. That was the past. I really do think that you should have told me about that night, but that's not important right now. We have to save my son's life."

"So what do we have to do?" Kevin asked.

Everyone turned to look at the doctor, who quickly explained that Kevin would have to first go through the same process that Marcus and Sasha had gone through. Marcus only heard the first couple of words before he zoned out to when Sahmeer was just a baby crawling around the house trying to play with everything. He snapped back out of it a minute later.

"We really need a match right now, and there's no one better than you. So can you just get tested to make sure, and we'll sort all of this out later?" he told Kevin.

Kevin agreed, then went with the doctor to see if he was indeed a match. Mike was confused about the whole situation. He needed to get out of there, so while everyone was talking, he slipped out of the hospital. Sasha looked around for him because she wanted to give him an explanation, but didn't see him. She and Akiylah stayed by Sahmeer, waiting for the results. Kevin ended up being a perfect match, and they immediately performed the transfusion.

Akiylah informed Sasha that she needed to go home to change her clothes and that she would be back soon. Sasha gave her the car keys and told her to bring something to eat back.

An hour later and after a successful transfusion, both Sahmeer and Kevin were sleeping peacefully. Sasha decided to stay, so Marcus left because he needed to get some air. He had some calls to make also, so he got in his car and left the hospital.

~ ~ ~ ~

Akiylah arrived at the house and parked. There were so many questions going through her head, but right now she just needed a hot shower and some fresh clothing to wear. One thing she was sure of was that she didn't have to worry about being poor anymore. She walked in, kicked off her shoes, and proceeded upstairs to her and Sahmeer's bedroom. After undressing, she went into the bathroom and turned on the shower. She checked the temperature, then got in. The water was so soothing to her skin. She closed her eyes and enjoyed the sensation of the water as it ran down her body.

Someone walked into the bathroom and just stood there watching her. He took off his clothes and stood by the sink, massaging his penis. Once it was fully hard, he walked over toward the shower and opened the door. Akiylah jumped, but once she saw who it was, a smile crept across her face.

"Me been waiting for you, baby," she said.

"Oh, is that right?" he replied, stepping inside and closing the door behind him.

Akiylah gave him a passionate kiss while rubbing his erection. He squeezed her ass cheeks, then turned her around. She arched her back, anticipating him entering her from behind. Not being able to hold back any longer, he entered her moist love box. She let out a soft moan, which almost caused him to ejaculate instantly.

"Me love you dick. It feels so good," she purposefully whined while moving her hips trying to match each stroke.

"Oh, is that right? Well then say my name," he replied, pumping in and out of her.

She was so caught up in the moment that she didn't hear a word he said to her. She was on the brink of getting her orgasm, when he stopped mid stroke.

"I said, say my name before I cum all over your ass," he repeated, trying to talk dirty to her and yanking her hair back.

Wanting him to continue so she could reach her climax, she said his name.

"Mike, please just keep fucking me."

BOOKS BY GOOD2GO AUTHORS

GOOD 2 GO FILMS PRESENTS

To order books, please fill out the order form below:

To order films please go to **www.good2gofilms.com**

Name:_____

Address:_____

City: _____ State: _____ Zip Code: _____

Phone:_____

Email:_____

Method of Payment: Check   VISA   MASTERCARD

Credit Card#:_____

Name as it appears on card: _____

Signature: _____

Item Name	Price	Qty	Amount
48 Hours to Die – Silk White	$14.99		
A Hustler's Dream - Ernest Morris	$14.99		
A Hustler's Dream 2 - Ernest Morris	$14.99		
Business Is Business – Silk White	$14.99		
Business Is Business 2 – Silk White	$14.99		
Business Is Business 3 – Silk White	$14.99		
Childhood Sweethearts – Jacob Spears	$14.99		
Childhood Sweethearts 2 – Jacob Spears	$14.99		
Childhood Sweethearts 3 - Jacob Spears	$14.99		
Childhood Sweethearts 4 - Jacob Spears	$14.99		
Flipping Numbers – Ernest Morris	$14.99		
Flipping Numbers 2 – Ernest Morris	$14.99		
He Loves Me, He Loves You Not - Mychea	$14.99		
He Loves Me, He Loves You Not 2 - Mychea	$14.99		
He Loves Me, He Loves You Not 3 - Mychea	$14.99		
He Loves Me, He Loves You Not 4 – Mychea	$14.99		
He Loves Me, He Loves You Not 5 – Mychea	$14.99		
Lord of My Land – Jay Morrison	$14.99		
Lost and Turned Out – Ernest Morris	$14.99		
Married To Da Streets – Silk White	$14.99		
M.E.R.C. - Make Every Rep Count Health and Fitness	$14.99		
My Besties – Asia Hill	$14.99		
My Besties 2 – Asia Hill	$14.99		
My Besties 3 – Asia Hill	$14.99		
My Besties 4 – Asia Hill	$14.99		
My Boyfriend's Wife - Mychea	$14.99		
My Boyfriend's Wife 2 – Mychea	$14.99		
Naughty Housewives – Ernest Morris	$14.99		
Naughty Housewives 2 – Ernest Morris	$14.99		
Naughty Housewives 3 – Ernest Morris	$14.99		
Never Be The Same – Silk White	$14.99		
Stranded – Silk White	$14.99		
Slumped – Jason Brent	$14.99		

Tears of a Hustler - Silk White	$14.99		
Tears of a Hustler 2 - Silk White	$14.99		
Tears of a Hustler 3 - Silk White	$14.99		
Tears of a Hustler 4- Silk White	$14.99		
Tears of a Hustler 5 – Silk White	$14.99		
Tears of a Hustler 6 – Silk White	$14.99		
The Panty Ripper - Reality Way	$14.99		
The Panty Ripper 3 – Reality Way	$14.99		
The Solution – Jay Morrison	$14.99		
The Teflon Queen – Silk White	$14.99		
The Teflon Queen 2 – Silk White	$14.99		
The Teflon Queen 3 – Silk White	$14.99		
The Teflon Queen 4 – Silk White	$14.99		
The Teflon Queen 5 – Silk White	$14.99		
The Teflon Queen 6 - Silk White	$14.99		
The Vacation – Silk White	$14.99		
Tied To A Boss - J.L. Rose	$14.99		
Tied To A Boss 2 - J.L. Rose	$14.99		
Tied To A Boss 3 - J.L. Rose	$14.99		
Time Is Money - Silk White	$14.99		
Two Mask One Heart – Jacob Spears and Trayvon Jackson	$14.99		
Two Mask One Heart 2 – Jacob Spears and Trayvon Jackson	$14.99		
Two Mask One Heart 3 – Jacob Spears and Trayvon Jackson	$14.99		
Young Goonz – Reality Way	$14.99		
Young Legend – J.L. Rose	$14.99		
Subtotal:			
Tax:			
Shipping (Free) U.S. Media Mail:			
Total:			

Make Checks Payable To:
Good2Go Publishing
7311 W Glass Lane,
Laveen, AZ 85339